NOTHING. NOTHING. nothing nothing NOTHING. Nothing THING. nothing THING. NOTHING Nothing NOTHING hing. nothing. Nothing. NOTHING THING NOTHING NOTHING THING. NOTHING. NOTHIN NOTHING NoTHING. Not nothing. nothing. NOTHING nothing. GNOTHING. NOTHING NOTHING. NOTHING

ANNIE BARROWS

NOTHING

GREENWILLOW BOOKS

AN IMPRINT OF HARPERCOLLINSPUBLISHERS

The text of this book is set in Joanna MT Std.

Book design by Sylvie Le Floc'h

Library of Congress Cataloging-in-Publication Data is available.

ISBN 978-0-06-266823-3 (hardback)

ISBN 978-0-06-279651-6 (ANZ)

17 18 19 20 21 PC/LSCH 10 9 8 7 6 5 4 3 2 1

First Edition

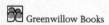 Greenwillow Books

For Esme,

obviously

NOTHING

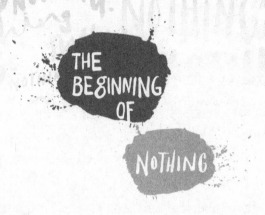

THE BEGINNING OF NOTHING

"Nothing," said Charlotte.

"A blank book, you mean?" said Frankie. She stuffed her phone between the couch cushions and rolled over on her back. "Hater. We're not that lame."

"No. Not blank. Just, like, boring," Charlotte said. "If you wrote a book about our real lives, nothing would happen. Ever." She tossed the book she was reading over the side of the couch and slid down, wedging her feet into Frankie's armpit.

"Get out," Frankie said, slapping her foot halfheartedly.

"Shut up." Charlotte dug her feet deeper into Frankie's armpit and resumed talking. "In there"—she waved at the book on the floor—"the main girl has red ringlets, like, three feet long—"

"Bitch."

"And everyone thinks she's hot but she doesn't care, because she has a *secret*."

"Ooh-ooh, a *secret*," snickered Frankie. "This is why I don't read."

"Guess what it is."

"Get your feet out of my armpit first," said Frankie.

"Guess," commanded Charlotte.

"Rape, incest," said Frankie in a bored voice. "Or oh my god, she's gay."

"Oh my god, she's gay," said Charlotte. "And then oh my god, there's a rainstorm and oh my god, she doesn't have an umbrella, so she runs into a—wait for it—"

"An AA meeting!" yelled Frankie.

"No! A sculpture class!" said Charlotte. "Where she sees a gorgeous Iranian girl with oh my god, scars on her wrists, and they exchange stares of attraction."

"Yeah, yeah," said Frankie. "Where's the dead mom?"

"Dead brother. Iranian girl's."

"Her fault?"

"Duh."

"Is there a scene where the main girl runs through a storm to save the Iranian girl from suicide and they touch each other and then have insane sex?"

Charlotte wrinkled her nose. "No storm. There was already a rainstorm when they met. They can't have two rainstorms."

"But suicide and insane sex?"

"Yeah. The sex part's good." With a grunt, Charlotte propelled herself halfway off the couch to retrieve the book.

"Oh god! Get your gross feet out of my face!" wailed Frankie.

Returning to the couch with a thump, Charlotte flipped through the book. "Here. Page two hundred eleven." She passed it down the couch.

Frankie read breathily, " ' "No," I whispered. I meant yes. Yesyesyes. She knew. She knew everything. She knew how to slide her cool hands under me, she knew how to open my legs—' " Frankie fell silent, reading. "Whoo-whoo, that is hot." After a moment, she looked up at Charlotte with shining eyes. "Why aren't we gay?"

"I know," said Charlotte. "But we're not. At least, I'm not. I don't know about you. You seem a little gay to me."

"You know what would be really good?" said Frankie dreamily. "If one of us was gay and, like, dying of secret lust for the other. And then there could be a discovery scene. And then insane sex."

"Sorry," said Charlotte. "Not going to happen. 'Cause we're not gay. We like disgusting smelly guys who don't like us. Like Kellen and Reed. Fuckers."

"Fuckers," Frankie agreed.

"And," continued Charlotte, "even if we were gay, probably no one would like us. Look at Noony. It's not like she's having nights of insane sex. She's having nights of insane homework, same as us."

"Nights of homework, days of school, weekends of hanging around wishing that something would happen. And sometimes—yay!—babysitting!" Frankie tossed the book back to the floor. "Now I feel all shitty. Reading sucks."

"We suck," said Charlotte.

A distant slam. "I'm *home*!" Heels sounded heavily in the hallway, and Charlotte's mother thumped into the kitchen. She was much smaller than her footsteps suggested. She looked suspiciously at the girls on the couch. "You haven't been eating my lettuce, have you?"

"Hi, Charlotte," said Charlotte. "How was school?"

"You look like you might have been eating my lettuce."

Charlotte rolled her eyes at Frankie. "Most moms worry that their kids are getting into the liquor cabinet. My mom worries that I ate lettuce."

"My lettuce," her mom clarified. "The liquor's right up there." She pointed to a high cupboard. "Oh shit. Sorry." She glanced worriedly at Frankie. "I shouldn't say stuff like that. Just kidding! Don't drink, kids!"

"Mom!" groaned Charlotte.

"Okay, okay. I'll go change," said her mom. "Don't do drugs!" She clomped away.

Charlotte winced. "She's a weirdo."

Frankie nodded. "But still: the eccentric mother. At least you've got that."

Charlotte laughed. "Nah. Only grandmas get to be eccentric. Moms in books are either dead or drunk."

"Nuh-uh. I've read ones where the mom is all life-forcey and wacky."

"Those ones die," Charlotte pointed out.

"Oh yeah. Right."

"The thing is, real life isn't *about* anything. That's what I meant," Charlotte said. Frankie looked a question. "You know, when I said that a book about our lives would be about nothing. There wouldn't be a plot, because we do the same stuff every day."

"No wild sex, either," said Frankie glumly.

Charlotte shook her head. "Nobody our age actually has wild sex."

"Aaron Shields does. He says."

Charlotte rolled her eyes. "No one he's doing it with says so. You know Lena? She said never again. So, okay: no plot, no sex, and no character development, because everyone's exactly the same as they've always been."

"Hey!" Frankie kicked her. "I've changed a lot!" She frowned. "Haven't I?"

Charlotte snorted. "You wish. I've known you since you were eight, and you haven't changed at all."

"You have. You're more of a bitch."

"Shut up."

Frankie pulled her phone out from the cushions and looked at it. "Check out my ratio," she said, holding out her phone.

Charlotte glanced at the phone. "Groovy." Then came a long period of silence while Frankie liked photos and Charlotte gazed out the window.

"Look—" Frankie held out the phone again. "She's wearing that V neck you almost got. I hate that color."

"Yeah." Charlotte nodded absently. "You know, I'm going to do it."

"What? The V neck? I don't—"

"No. The book. I'm going to write a book about what our lives are really like," said Charlotte. "I'm going to make it my senior project."

"You're only a sophomore," said Frankie.

"I'll get it done early."

Frankie screwed up her face. "But nothing ever happens to us."

"I know!" said Charlotte excitedly. "That's the point! It'll be, like, a searing document of today's youth and how incredibly boring our lives are!"

Frankie paused. "Am I going to be in it?"

"Hello? You're my best friend. You have to be in it. This is a true story."

"Can't you make something happen to me?"

"Nuh-uh! Only the truth!"

Frankie groaned. "Oh my god, I'm bored already."

"Too bad, Franklin."

"Fuck me," said Frankie.

And that was how Nothing began.

NOTHING

"Fuck me," sighed Frankie.

Frankie is my best friend. People are always saying that they're best friends or BFFs or mains, and it makes me want to scream because then they turn around and talk shit about each other or say it about someone else or whatever. I hate that.

I bet you think I'm going to follow that up by saying But not me and Frankie. We're the real deal. We've got each other's back, through thick and thin, fire and rain, blah blah blah.

Bullshit.

I mean, I love Frankie, I really do. She's been my best friend since we were eight, except for a little while in seventh grade when this bitch Ohndie stole her. I'm still mad about that. But Frankie's funny and smart and she actually listens to other people and thinks about what they say, but no one besides me really knows that because she doesn't talk much. She can be intense, though. Maybe I really mean determined. She wants to get on with it. Like one time when we were little, Frankie's dad took us rock climbing—not serious rock climbing, kid rock climbing. Still, I was scared. I got on this ledge and I wanted to stay there until I wasn't scared anymore. Frankie stayed there next to me, but it made her crazy. She kept saying, "It's okay. It's okay. I'll stay with you," and then she couldn't stand it anymore, and she just dang jumped off that ledge. I almost had a heart attack and so did her dad. Why am I telling this story? Oh yeah, to show that Frankie's intense. She used to be, anyway. Now she spends most of her time on the phone. I'm not blaming her, because I do, too. Everyone does. There's not that much else to do.

There's this unspoken—what? Idea, I guess—among all grown-ups that teenagers are bums. That all we care about is social media and it's giving us brain cancer and making us dumb and we'll never get jobs and we'll end up living in our parents' basements. So we feel guilty every time they see us look at our phones, but the whole thing is fucked up because what else are we supposed to do?

My dad is all, "You should be helping the less fortunate."

But I do! I'm in Social Action Club at school! We fill grocery bags at the food bank and stuff. They won't let us actually hand out food to homeless people because of their insurance. I suppose I could go to St. Vincent's and serve dinner, but I don't know how I'd get there and I guess I would be kind of scared to go alone. I pick up garbage at the beach three times a year, too.

What else can I do? Get a job? I wish, 'cause I'm broke, but what job? Not even grown-ups can get jobs. Is there a job I can get on Sunday from noon to five? Because that's all the time I've got left over after school and orchestra (which my parents won't let me quit) and track (which they also won't let me quit).

My mom thank god doesn't say things like I should be helping the less fortunate, but I know what she's thinking. She's thinking I'm not creative. I know this because every time I happen to mention by mistake that I'm bored, she yells, "Make something! Do something! Be something!"

And I want to yell back (but I don't) "Like *what*?" Because realistically, what can I do? Nothing. I'm not allowed to. I can't drive. I can't even start learning to drive until I'm fifteen and a half, and even if I could, I couldn't go anywhere with my friends (you can only drive with grown-ups until you've had your license for a year). My parents would never let me go out into nature by myself. They won't even let me go to the city, unless I tell them exactly where I'm going and I'm home by six. And no matter what, I have to be at school at eight o'clock every morning, so it's not like can go out and have *adventures*. What I'd really like to do? Go on a road trip to see this friend of mine named Sid who lives in Oregon. But is that going to happen? No. It isn't. Because how could it? (And let me just say right now that I'm not going to explain who Sid is. It's completely ridiculous.)

The reality is, my parents are kind of hypocrites. Not in an evil way—they don't pretend to be religious and then screw teenagers or anything—but in the way that grown-ups almost always are. They say they want me to do things and be creative, but they really don't. Or they only want me to do things that are totally safe and not too expensive and don't mess up the house and don't interfere with homework and don't cause me to be late for dinner. Which pretty much reduces my options to zero.

I first noticed this little hypocrisy problem of theirs when I was eight. What happened was, I read this amazing, fantastic book about a kid who spied on all her neighbors, and I was like, Hallelujah! I have found my calling! I'm going to be a spy! I figured I should start training right away, so I got together this whole notebook and special outfit, and I went around my block, spying on people and writing down what they did. Sometimes I even tiptoed down their driveways to see what was happening in their backyards. I found out a bunch of weird stuff, too. Like this old lady neighbor of ours, her house looks fine from the front, but if you go in the backyard— hoarder! But then Totally Uptight Clay caught me in his garage and *freaked* and told my parents, and they called me into the dining room to have a big Behavior Talk. I was just a little kid, so I cried and promised them I'd never spy again. But the truth is, I got in trouble for being creative.

This is the kind of stuff that turns you cynical.

But I love my parents. I love them like crazy. So I'm a good kid, and I do the things they want me to do, and I don't mention to them that they're hypocrites, and everyone's happy. Except when they say, "Make something! Do something! Be something!" and I get pissed.

But ha! I am realizing right this second that writing a book about Nothing *is* creative. Take that, Mom! I'm being creative!

I'm probably not going to tell her, though. She'd want to read it.

[Break here because I was checking my phone—so kill me, I had to ask Maia H. if we were supposed to do problems one to twenty or the whole page. My geometry teacher is a complete dick and won't write the homework on the board or put it up on his site because he says we should be paying attention when he says it. Which I would be if I could *hear* him, but I can't because I sit between Worried Alex and Dominic. Worried Alex is always talking to himself because he has anxiety, and Dominic is always talking because he's an asshole. So I have to ask around, which is a lot harder than you'd think since most people don't give a shit about me getting the homework. Except Maia H., who's a really nice girl. A little on the dull side, but nice. And after that, I had a bunch of texts from: Noony, Noony, Gaby, Noony, Sid, Alex (not Worried Alex, a different Alex), Johnny Game (not as cool as he sounds), Noony, Sid, Gaby, Eden, Eden, Frankie (even though she's here), Alex, Alex, Reed (!) (but it was stupid), Kellen, Kellen, Alex, Noony. Noony has an emoji addiction. Then Frankie showed me this picture she'd just gotten from this guy Soren, which was him without a shirt, and she says Are you actually sending me nudes, you creep? And he says Devon stole his phone and sent the picture to her. And then she says Why are you getting naked with Devon? And then he got really mad and she felt bad. I told her not to send it.]

I don't know why I put all that in brackets. That's the Nothing this book is about. I just noticed that I've written 1,429 words (yay, Word Count!) and I still haven't finished what I started to say about Frankie and me.

So. Frankie and me.

Frankie and Me: The Friendship.

Ah, fuck it. You'll figure it out.

I think I'll write about how we look instead.

Frankie first. Frankie's gorgeous. [Shut up, Frankie. You *are*.] Everyone thinks Frankie's gorgeous because of her hair—it's long and super-dark, almost black, and way silky—but if you really look at her, you realize that she's gorgeous because of how her face and her hair look together. Her skin is really pale and her hair is really dark and the contrast is amazing. She looks like a vampire, in a good way. Sometimes we do her makeup to emphasize that—we darken her brows and put on blood-red lipstick and pull her hair back to show she's got a heart-shaped face. I think it looks great. She thinks she looks like Morticia, at least that's what she says, but she puts the pictures up and someone always says Suck mine and then, I meant neck!

I would say—just keeping it real here—that her brows are her worst feature. They're different shapes. One is kind of weirdly square, and the other is arched. We can make it better, but unlike lashes, you're really kind of stuck with your brows. Frankie has this friend, Merle—oh my god, I don't even want to talk about Merle. She's perfect. Beyond. She has fucking long legs and fucking perfect brows and long curly hair and when I stand next to her, I am a misshapen dwarf.

Anyway, Frankie would say [I know because I just asked her] that her entire body is her worst feature. She's insane. She's tall, which I would kill for, and thin, which I would also kill for [pause for an argument about me not being thin] and she's built like a model.

"Also an ironing board," yells Frankie. "And a guy. Except that I'm taller than most guys, and no one's ever going to have sex with me. Put that in."

And my father walks into the kitchen. "Hi, girls," he booms.

"Hi, Dad," I say. Frankie is busy turning red because he might have heard her say the word sex, so she jumps up from the sofa and starts shuffling around with her papers and folders, which are scattered all over the floor. "I should get going," she says, still red.

"Don't mind me," Dad says, frowning. He thinks she's leaving because he came in.

"Oh no!" Frankie says, trying to sound like she isn't. "My dad said I had to be home at—whoa!" She's blinking at her phone. "Five thirty."

Dad looks at his watch. "It's six fifteen."

I stand up, too—Frankie gets in trouble if she's really late, which this is on the brink of being—and help her get her stuff together. Then we hug and she goes tearing out of the house. Usually I go tearing out with her;

[first semicolon! I don't really understand what they do] sometimes I even go all the way to her house, which is only four blocks away but uphill. Today, though, I don't. It's because of Nothing. I'm kind of having fun. Plus, I want to write about how I look.

Frankie Tries to Keep Her Parents Happy and Doesn't Exactly Succeed

Frankie was in the doghouse. It wasn't the worst place to be—it wasn't, for instance, like being grounded or defunded (that's what her parents called no allowance) or having her phone taken away. The doghouse was just a place of disapproval. But disapproval, Frankie knew, could grow into something bigger. Disapproval was a building block of trouble. Right now, at the dinner table, her mom and dad were being overly polite to her. It was a bad sign. She would have to start doing her homework the second she finished dinner—that would soften them up.

"Can I have some more salad?" she asked strategically. Her

mom loved her more when she ate vegetables.

"Sure, honeybun," her mom replied, scraping back her chair.

"She can get it," said her dad in a friendly yet warning voice.

Frankie took the hint. "Yeah, Mom, I'll get it." She took her bowl to the kitchen and filled it with salad.

"So what were you and Char up to this afternoon?" her mom asked as she returned to the dining room.

"That took so long," added her dad. Her mom shot him a don't-be-a-hardass look and turned back to Frankie.

"Nothing," answered Frankie truthfully. She tried to think of something to add. Conversations were the key to parental happiness. For a second, she considered telling them Charlotte's idea. But no. They'd want to read it. "We did some homework, but I have more. We talked about this dumb book Char read. We looked at some pictures. You know." This, she could tell from their faces, was not an impressive list. She searched her brainpan for further unclassified information. "Ms. Barbaneri said today that most people in the world think that the United States bombed the two towers itself. You know, the 9/11 towers."

"That is the most ridiculous misconception ever," her dad began.

"She wasn't saying *she* believed it. She was saying that most of the rest of the world does," explained Frankie hurriedly. She didn't want him going off on Ms. Barbaneri, who was nice.

"I know, I know, but it's a completely skewed vision of the reality of the United States," her father said, his voice rising. "It's just that these people have no tradition of democracy or transparency, no government worthy of the name, so this kind of moronic idea gains currency among an uneducated populace."

"But, you know, it's sort of, um, a compliment," Frankie said. "Because it's like they think we're, like, evil magicians or something."

"It's not a compliment!" her dad said. "Not when they use it as an excuse to kill innocent people!"

"That's not what I meant," began Frankie.

But now her mom interrupted. "Tommy. What I think Frankie meant was that it's a compliment that they think our government is so powerful that it could sustain a conspiracy like that. Is that what you were saying, honey?"

Frankie nodded. Forget it.

There was a silence.

"How was English?" asked her mom. "Did she control the class today?"

Frankie winced. "Sort of."

"Do you want me to call? I can call." Her mom looked at her searchingly.

Frankie shrugged. "It's okay. It was a little better today."
It had, actually, been a nightmare, with Miss Mathers holding
her hands over her ears and squeaking, "Ooh, it's too noisy,
ooh, my head." What a moron. She should just tell Chris and
Chris to shut the hell up. Or send them out of the room or
something.

Still, she didn't want her mom to call. Frankie was a
hundred percent sure—no matter what anyone said—that
Miss Mathers would find out it was her mom who complained.
And once she found out, Miss Mathers would start making
little comments like, "Frankie, isn't all this noise terrible?"
Or, "Chris, you need to apologize to Frankie for disturbing
her." Because underneath the ooh-ooh squeaking, Miss
Mathers hated them all. Hated them, as in would love to kill
them with her bare hands. Every day, her class was mayhem.
Out of control. No one learned anything. Miss Mathers dealt
with that by telling herself it wasn't her fault—her students
were animals; they were unteachable. But if she ever had even
the slightest chance of turning the mayhem against someone
other than herself, she'd take it. In a heartbeat, even if it was
the weirdest, saddest kid in class, like OCD Luis or Raven
(also known as Raven Nuts) because at least then, it wouldn't
be her.

Frankie knew she was not a likely candidate for being
turned against. She was a little popular, but not so popular

that she was secretly resented. Still, even if just a few of them turned against her, it would be bad. Especially if two of the few were Chris and Chris.

"Really, I'd be glad to call," her mother said again.

"No. Thanks. But no," Frankie said. She smiled at her mother. "Thanks anyway. I'd better do the rest of my stuff." She stood.

"What do you have?" her father asked casually.

"Just a little bit of reading and some notes," she answered, also casually.

"Like, how much reading?"

"Like, a chapter."

"Like, how long is this chapter?"

"Like, sixteen pages."

"That's a lot. Do you really think that spending two-and-a-half hours at Charlotte's was the best use of your time?"

"Probably not," answered Frankie.

"So?" asked her father.

"She gets it, hon," said her mom. "Why don't we just let her do her work?"

Thank you, Mom, Frankie said silently, moving toward her computer. And thank you, Dad, for pointing out my total irresponsibility, because otherwise I might have thought I was doing something good by starting my homework now. Jesus Christ. A whispered conversation arose behind her.

Her mom was trying to defuse her dad. Good luck with that, Mom, thought Frankie.

"Are you sure you're really learning what you're supposed to be learning with those headphones on?" her dad asked.

Frankie took the headphones off and continued reading.

"It was a question," her dad said. "Not an order."

"Okay. I took them off."

Her father looked almost helpless for a second. "Okay." Then he turned and went to sit in front of his own computer, across the room.

Frankie read. *Without governments to keep order, Hobbes believed that there would be a war of every man against every man. Hobbes called the agreement by which people gave up individual rights in exchange for law and order, **the social contract**.* "Hobbes," she wrote, "invented the social contract." Invented was the wrong word. Oh well. She knew what she meant.

Far off, she could hear her mother doing something quiet in the kitchen. From across the room came the dry tapping of keys.

Otherwise, nothing.

You want Nothing, Char, come to my house. This house is the capital of Nothing.

It wasn't like she wanted other parents, Frankie thought. Her parents were fine—her mom was great, and her dad was kind of neurotic but basically a good guy. You average that out and get fine. But it was so quiet.

It was like being an only child.

Frankie was not an only child. Put everyone together, and she was the youngest of five. Putting everyone together had been a big problem, though. Frankie's mother and father had been married to other people when they fell in love. In fact— this part had been completely breezed over when Frankie was little—they had been neighbors. The two families had been close friends: Frankie's mom, Sharon, and her first husband, Jasper, along with their two daughters, Lucy and Cate, had had barbeques and picnics and birthday parties with their neighbors, Tom and Bix, and their two boys, Leland and Max. Frankie had first gotten wind of this aspect of her parents' life during a major blowup between Leland and her dad when she was about seven. She couldn't remember what they'd been arguing about, but she remembered Leland screaming, "You want me to spell it out for you, Dad? Here you go: B-E-T-R-A-Y-A-L! Got that? *Betrayal.*" Frankie, two rooms away at her little art table, carefully wrote out the letters. Cate, sitting beside her at the table, glanced over at Frankie's paper.

"You wanna know what it means, Love Child?" Love Child was something Cate called her when her parents weren't around.

"Shut up, Cate," said Lucy, doing homework at the counter.

"Shut up yourself," snapped Cate. "She's going to find out sometime."

Lucy sighed. "Don't be mean about it, though, okay? It's not her fault." Lucy was always nice. Weirdly Christian, but nice.

"I'll be a lot nicer about it than Lee would be," said Cate. Which was almost certainly true. Leland was scary-nervy. Sometimes he was fun, but you could never tell when he'd go too far, laugh too loud, do something too crazy. He said things that everyone pretended he hadn't.

"He's just angry, honey," Frankie's mom had said once.

"But I didn't do anything," moaned Frankie, still crying. He'd made fun of her ballerina costume—he'd called her the capitalist fairy Fuckall in the Ballet of the First-World Pigs.

"No, you didn't," her mom agreed. "I did."

Everyone was relieved when Leland left for college, and even though he didn't stay in College #1 or College #2, he didn't come back home, either. Frankie was glad. But then Lucy went away to college, and Frankie wasn't glad about that. She missed Lucy's niceness, the way she did Frankie's hair in French braids, the way she patiently led her through cat's cradle and origami and other mysteries. But the main reason Frankie missed Lucy was that she was left alone with Cate, the Queen of Mean, and Silent Max.

Cate wasn't like Leland. She didn't yell or laugh too loud

or get wild. She just waited. She waited until you were weak, or you had made a mistake, or you had claimed too much— and then she pounced on you and ripped you apart. Mostly, she pounced on Frankie's mom. Sometimes on Frankie's dad. As often as she could, on Frankie. Almost never, on Silent Max.

When she was younger, Frankie thought Cate left Max alone because she liked him best, but later, she decided it was because there wasn't enough to pounce on. He never claimed anything, and if he made a mistake, he was so calm about it that Cate was left without any pain to make worse. One time he had been carrying a full pot of hot coffee through the kitchen when Frankie's aunt Grace had opened the refrigerator door right in front of him. He had tripped over her and broken the coffeepot *inside* the refrigerator, so that hot coffee flooded over everything. He stood there, dripping coffee and blood (he'd cut himself on the coffeepot), and all he said was, "Whoa. What a mess. Sorry." Then he'd calmly wrapped up his hand and cleaned the inside of the refrigerator, while everyone else screamed and ran around. When he was done, he unwrapped his hand and said, "Uh. I think I might need stitches." Twelve, to be exact. And he wasn't trying to keep calm. He just was calm.

He'd been the last to go, right when Frankie was about to start high school. She hadn't really expected to miss him, because he was, after all, Silent Max. He didn't say much or, as far as she could see, do much. But once she was at Arteaga High, she found out that he'd had a secret life. He wasn't one of the popular kids, but people had liked him. Of course, they weren't her crew; they were weirdos and music nerds, but even a few cool kids had acknowledged her because of Max. "You're McCullough's sister?" a hot junior had said, first week of her freshman year. He wiggled his eyebrows. "Not bad." Frankie had practically fainted. He'd never said anything to her again, but it had been a nice ten seconds.

And at home, at least there had been someone else around, another kid. Sometimes they'd made faces at each other when Dad was freaking, quick little oh-my-god faces. She missed it.

It was strange, too, how much quieter the house was without Silent Max. For two people who'd been so overwhelmed with passion that they'd destroyed six entire lives to be together, her mom and dad were incredibly dull. It wasn't that they didn't love each other anymore—Frankie caught them smooching all the time, which was kind of gross but reassuring. It was more like they had had enough excitement for a lifetime. Frankie snuck a glance at her father, bathed in blue computer light. He seemed mesmerized by the Excel worksheet on his screen. This is what he likes, Frankie thought. This is his big reward for all that craziness: control and quiet and everything being the same all the time.

Save me.

She turned back to her textbook and tried to focus. *The philosopher John Locke maintained a more positive view of human nature, believing that people could learn from experience and improve themselves.* You go, John. Frankie underlined *learn from experience and improve themselves.* More optimistic than whatsisname. Frankie looked at the previous paragraph—Hobbes. Hey! Calvin and Hobbes! Whoops. Concentration breakdown. Frankie pressed her hands on either side of her head to hold the information in. Hobbes: people are so shitty they shouldn't be allowed to make their own decisions. Locke: people can get less shitty, so they should be allowed to make decisions. Got it. She decided she was a Lockean. Lockite? She liked the positive attitude: People can get less shitty. Heck—she thought of school—they'd *better* get less shitty. Frankie looked down at herself. I'd better get less shitty, too. Change? Gladly. Bring on those learning experiences. Bring on that self-improvement. Yeah, right. She had to bring them on herself. She looked at her textbook without seeing it. Tomorrow, she resolved. Tomorrow I'll talk to Kellen instead of being a tongue-tied lame-o freak when he's around. Ta-da! I will be less shitty, starting tomorrow! Pleased with herself, she looked over at her father and his glowing worksheet. Okay, so she'd die of boredom if she were him, but at least he had gone for it once. He and her mom both. They could have stayed married to Jasper and Bix, but they'd taken the nuclear option, and now they had the incredibly boring lives they'd always dreamed of. Maybe not so hot for Jasper and Bix. But for Frankie's parents, it had been good. They'd taken action and improved their lives. They'd done something.

So will I.

Take that, Char. You Nothing-ist.

"Wow," murmured her father, staring in fascination at his worksheet.

NOTHING

So I never got around to saying what I look like because right after Frankie left, Maia H. got back to me and fuck me, it *was* the whole page we were supposed to do for math. So I got on that, and I swear to God I'd understand a lot more if I sat somewhere else. I had to *call* Maia H. halfway through, but like I said, she's really nice and she didn't mind.

"Look," she says, super-patiently, "look at the formula ABC equals b times h times one-half. Okay?"

"Yeah," I say, but not like I mean it.

"Do it. While I'm here. Plug in the numbers and tell me what you get." God, she's a saint.

I plug in some numbers. "Six?"

"Right," she says. "Now put that in c over 2r equals h over a."

Ohhh. Oh, I get it. I say this.

"Put the numbers in," she says. "I'll wait."

I put the numbers in. "A equals eighteen?"

"But you gotta divide it, remember? 'Cause you divided out the two from 2r."

"Aah, right. Nine."

"Right."

"Oh my god, you're a saint, Maia. Thank you so much, thank you—"

She's such a saint that she doesn't even want to hear about how great she is. "Call me if you need more help," she says, and hangs up.

Maybe she's religious or something. Maybe she's helping the meek—that would be me—because god told her to. Whatever. I love you, Maia.

After that I had to be Dad's servant while he made dinner. Dad likes cooking, but what he really likes is telling other people to bring him the lemons and chop those onions and wash off this spatula while he stands at the stove and stirs stuff. Am I making him sound like a dick? He's not. He's actually kind of noble because he's a lawyer for juvenile offenders, which means he spends most of his time with complete assholes, trying to save their asshole lives. He doesn't talk about it much because he's not allowed to, but every once in a while, he says something like "Do you know a kid named Brendan Scofield?" I say yeah, and he says, "Don't ever eat anything he gives you." And then, for the rest of my life, I can't stop staring at Brendan, wondering, What the hell did you *do*?

Dinner was Dad's famous fart pasta with broccoli and garbanzo beans, which I can't believe I eat even knowing what happens. My brother, Ollie—twelve, disgusting—eats tons of it on purpose. He starts farting right at the table, which is so gross I can't even stand it. "Why didn't you stop after me, Mom?" I moan. "Why didn't you quit while you were ahead?"

"I was talked into it," she says. "Your father dazzled me with his charm, and I lost my mind."

My dad farts.

"Possibly I was gassed," she says. Ollie farts some more, grinning. "In any case, it was a terrible mistake."

My mom is a little bit strange. Actually, I don't think she's strange. I think she's funny, but I realize that most people think she's weird. People my age, I mean. Even Frankie thinks some of the things she says are awful. Like if I repeated that thing about Ollie being a terrible mistake, Frankie'd freak. She'd think Ollie was going to be scarred for life or something. But Ollie knows Mom's joking. We all do. I used to try to tell my friends the things my parents say that crack me up, but I don't anymore. It doesn't translate.

Then after dinner, I was involved in major group-chat drama about this girl named Lisette who is, well, let's just say legend for getting wrecked and doing guys in weird places, for example under the bleachers during a soccer tournament. Go team. Anyway, everyone was piling on her for hooking up with this guy, Marin, who's supposed to be dating Serena Fong. Everyone was all, what a bitch, what a slut, what a ho. And so on. So I say, Why is no one blaming Marin, why is the girl a ho and the guy fine? You sexists. And then—oh, yay—132 texts denying that they're sexist, while still being sexist. I hate group chats.

Plus I still had reading to do.

Plus Sid usually texts me at around nine thirty.

Plus all the regular stuff like figuring out what to wear tomorrow and getting my backpack together and showering and zit control and my fucking teeth, which I'm not even going to talk about.

Here is Friday morning:

7:05: *Hey can you bring my plant shirt?*

7:06: *Yag cu* [Yag means yes. Inside joke.]

7:07–7:46: many boring things, including me walking to school

7:47–8:00: Frankie, red-faced from running, throws her backpack on the ground next to my feet. "Hi," she pants. "Is it in here?" She's rooting around in my backpack.

"Oh my GOD, don't mess everything up!" I yell, slapping at her. She keeps on messing everything up, so I yank my backpack away from her.

Except she won't let go, and she bonks me with her hip to knock me over.

"Here! Here!" I yell, holding out her shirt. "Jesus, you're such a bitch!"

She grabs it. "Thanks, sistah" and runs off to the bathroom to change, yelling, "Watch my stuff," over her shoulder. She almost runs into one of the Chrises, but doesn't at the last second, turns around to make a face at me about that, and actually does run into a guy named Dagoberto—not kidding—and practically kills him because he's like the size of a ten-year-old. And he gets all mad and starts screaming at her and she's apologizing but she's still running, too, because she's only got eight minutes before the bell rings.

And then Noony comes and she's having drama about her pants, which is like a daily occurrence because Noony's mom won't let her wear leggings to school. "She's all, No daughter of mine is going to leave this house looking like a slut, and I'm all, Mom, please, I'm gay, and she's all, I don't care, and then I say, You don't care 'cause you think it's a phase but it's not. I'm into girls, Mom. I want to make out with girls, Mom," she says, and I start laughing. [I wonder what it would be like to make out with Noony. Can't picture it. No, wait, I can. Bleee-yah. Besides, that would ruin my book.] Here comes Gaby. I give her a hug. And here's Eden, who's always a little bit out of it.

"Hey Eden, what's happening?"

"What?" That's how she answers everything. She's pretty, with far-apart eyes like a kitten. There's some weirdness about her family, but I don't know exactly what it is. I don't know that much about her at all, really. I always thought she was Gaby's best friend, but one time when I was having a sleepover with Gaby, I said that, and Gaby said she didn't know what I was talking about. She said she never hung out with Eden alone. I guess no one does.

And then Frankie came running back in her plant shirt. "Yeah?" she asked, modeling for me.

"Tuck it in."

She tucked it in.

"No, untuck it."

She untucked it.

"Cute."

"Hair up or down?"

"Down, down, completely down."

Then this girl I can't stand named Cora came over. She's so fake. I don't know why she has any friends at all. She's always doing this thing that drives me crazy, putting up super-posed pictures of herself standing at, like, the beach in a tiny bikini, with captions like, "Lil nature fairy—had to take a mental health day, had to see the sky. . . ." Shut the fuck up.

She's all fake-smiling at me. "Your jacket is so cute, I love it!" Then she puts her arm around me and takes a selfie, with peace sign, of course. And I have to pretend I'm so *happy* that she likes my jacket. Like I care.

Then that asshole Kellen comes over and starts leaning all over Cora, right in front of Frankie. What the fuck? He doesn't know Frankie likes him? He's a dick. And Cora's squealing, "Get away, get awaaaay."

Meanwhile Eden is staring into space. Gaby's texting Alex, who's late. Noony's doing math problems. Frankie's standing to one side, and then she gives me this little smile and mutters, "In one of those teen books, that would be a plot twist." She sort of nods at Cora and Kellen.

I look at them—Kellen leaning and Cora fake-squealing at him—and say, "In a teen book, some up-till-now-unnoticed guy would spill coffee on you right this second, and it would be the beginning of a huge thing."

And damn us, we can't help it. We look around for a guy with a coffee cup. Nothing. Nada. Bupkis. Real life doesn't have plot twists.

"Did anyone figure out the answer to number sixteen?" asks Noony.

8:01: The bell rings.

It's Friday.
Let the Excitement Begin

Frankie was trying, sincerely trying, not to look at the clock. 3:04. Come on, baby, she begged it. Shake your ass.

"I don't really get it," Davindra was saying to Miss Mathers. Which was all he ever said.

"Don't be la-aame, Daveeeendra," one of the Chrises yelled across the room.

Miss Mathers whirled around, her face pink. "I will not have anyone making fun of names in my class!"

"What? Whose name?" said the Chris, holding up his hands like he didn't understand what she was talking about. *"What?"*

"Who would like to explain to Chris what I mean?" she said. Oh god help us all, thought Frankie wearily. No one's going to say anything.

No one said anything.

"Well, then, you'll just stay right in your seats until someone can give Chris an explanation," said Miss Mathers in a satisfied voice.

"But the bell's about to ring," complained Marco.

"I have to go!" yelled Chloe. "I have a doctor's appointment!"

The other Chris said softly, "Aw, who's the father?"

Uproar.

"What? *What?*" "Nobody leaves until *both* of you apologize!" "I gotta go!" "Sorry, Miss Mathers, coach said!" "*What?* I don't get it!" "Shut up." "Shut up." "Shut up."

And then they were all getting up, shoving books in their backpacks, putting jackets on, taking out phones. Frankie, Josh, Luis, and Tara kept sitting, to make Miss Mathers feel better. Tara even said, "What's the homework again, Miss Mathers?" like nothing was happening. Miss Mathers jumped at the chance, too, and started gabbing about the homework, so that some of the leavers stopped leaving and listened, even though most didn't. Miss Mathers pretended like she hadn't told them to stay, and they pretended like she hadn't been disobeyed, and Frankie was only a couple minutes late to meet Charlotte.

"Thank GOD," Frankie said, leaping on her.

"Lester!" Charlotte caught her, and they whirled around, hugging. "It's Friday! It's Friday!" she sang.

"Shut up, shut up," Frankie sang back.

"Ow," Charlotte dropped her. "My back. Noony had to go help her grandma with something, but she said we should text her what we're doing and maybe she can meet up."

"What are we doing?" asked Frankie. Because it was December and therefore between cross-country and track seasons and therefore winter conditioning and therefore they didn't have practice on Friday, they could do whatever they wanted. Which was what?

A backpack came flying over Charlotte's head. "So—what are we doing?" It was Gaby.

They counted their money and waited around for Alex and then smoked Alex's weed and then waited around some more for Reed and then tried to decide between bubble tea and pizza and coffee and yogurt and burritos. Alex and Reed wanted burritos, so they walked to the burrito place, which was close to the bubble tea place, but Gaby wanted a chai, so they went to get that and then Noony texted, *where u?*, so they went up to Canyon, which was not a canyon but a rock, a big one, and sat around until Noony showed up.

Even though it was cold—California cold, not really cold—they stayed there until the sun set. Frankie leaned back against the granite, shivering a little in her hoodie. She envied Gaby, wrapped in Alex's arms. Though she herself would never in a million years date Alex. He was kind of dumb. She knew for a fact he'd thought Africa was a country until last year. She glanced over at Reed, who was pretending he was about to pour his Arizona on Charlotte. They had hooked up once at the beginning of the year, and he knew she liked him, so he was sort of flirting, and Charlotte was sort of halfheartedly squealing. Maybe she was over it. Frankie hoped so; they were never going to be a thing. And neither were she and Kellen—she admitted it. Her be-the-change-you-want-to-see resolution looked pretty worthless now. Kellen could get girls like Cora, and Frankie wasn't that. She took a quick look at herself in her camera and wished her boobs were bigger or the rest of her was smaller. Sometimes she thought she was pretty and sometimes she thought she was gross and sometimes—a lot of times—she just didn't know. Today she didn't know.

If she was being honest, Kellen was kind of dumb, too. He got good grades, but he had no idea what was going on. He was like, Syria? What about Syria? Jesus. And he had really bad taste in music. He liked Five Seconds of Summer. Charlotte had almost killed him when she found that out—she was all, "Only thirteen-year-old girls like 5-SOS, Kel. You can't like them." But he did anyway. At the time, Frankie had thought it was nice that he was so loyal, but now she thought maybe he just didn't know the names of any other bands.

Charlotte plopped down next to her. "Jesus Christ," she said under her breath, and Frankie knew she was talking about Reed.

"Not worth it," said Frankie.

"No shit," said Charlotte, burrowing close so that Frankie put her arm around her. "But look at Gaby and Alex. They're ruining my life."

"They hate each other. They told me," Frankie said, and Charlotte snickered.

"What are you guys doing?" It was Noony, sitting down behind them. "Let me in." They cuddled together, watching the sun set on the bay.

"Hey!" Reed turned on his little rock outcropping. "What the fuck? Everyone's hooking up but me! Gimme some!"

"Dream on," Noony muttered into Charlotte's neck.

"Dream on!" screeched Frankie and Charlotte in unison. They had an Aerosmith thing. Noony groaned. "Dream on! Sing with me, sing for the years!"

"Shut up!" Gaby yelled. "Oh my god, it's all your fault, Noony! Somebody stop them!"

"Sing for the laughter, sing for the tears!"

"Shut the fuck up!" yelled someone farther up the rock.

"Dream on!" screamed Frankie and Charlotte. But they were laughing too hard to sing more.

And then the sun set.

"Okay, sweetie, Daddy and I are going to bed," said Frankie's mom, brushing her hand through Frankie's hair.

Frankie almost fell off her stool. "Jesus! Heart attack! Mom!" She took her earbuds out.

Her mom rolled her eyes. "I was just saying good night. Dad and I are going to bed."

"Oh. Okay. G'night!" Frankie glanced at her phone. "It's only nine thirty."

"We're tired," her mom said. She yawned to prove it.

"Mom?"

"Frankie?"

"Can we practice driving during Christmas break?"

Her mother sighed deeply. "I don't know. Ask Dad."

Now it was Frankie's turn to sigh. "Okay." She paused. "He just gets so uptight about it."

"I know," her mom said. "I'll see if I can stand it." She glanced at Frankie's phone. "You texting Charlotte?"

Frankie nodded.

"Why don't you just hang out together?"

"If I could *drive*, I would. But right now, I don't feel like walking home in the cold at eleven thirty at night." Her mother smiled and turned to go. "Hey, Mom?" Her mother turned back. "When you were my age, did you have a boyfriend?"

Hesitation. "Yes."

"I knew it!" said Frankie. "I'm a loser."

"You are not!" Her mom leaped to her defense. "You're absolutely not. If all you wanted was just any boyfriend, you'd have one. You want a boyfriend you like."

Frankie shrugged. "The ones I like don't like me."

"Then they're idiots and they don't deserve you."

"Said my mom."

"Well, it's true! You might just have to wait until the guys are older and smarter."

"Great." Frankie sighed. "How old was the boyfriend you had when you were my age?"

"Senior."

"Oh my god! You went out with a *senior*?"

Her mom nodded.

"No senior would ever ask me out."

"That's crazy," her mother said. "I don't get that. When I was in high school, it was standard operating procedure for senior guys to go out with sophomore girls."

"Not now," said Frankie. "I guess it happens, but not a ton."

Her mom gave her a sly look. "After we broke up, when I was sixteen, I went out with a twenty-two-year-old."

"You did *not!*"

"I did. He was incredibly cute."

"You wild thing! Didn't Grandma freak?"

Her mom giggled. "She didn't know."

"You *sneaked?*" asked Frankie. "Mom!"

Her mom sat down on the next stool. "It wasn't exactly sneaking. Grandma knew where I was. She just didn't know he was there, too. It didn't last long anyway."

"Your life was way more exciting than mine is," Frankie said glumly.

"Eh." Her mom shrugged. "It wasn't that exciting. He was cute, but not much else. I just went out with him to prove I could."

"Prove to who?"

"To me. You know, to prove I could get him."

"And you did."

"But then we didn't have anything to talk about. Anyway, it wasn't much fun after the first part."

"Still," Frankie said. She waved a hand toward the empty kitchen. "Probably more fun than this."

Her mother patted her cheek. "You know what? You're going to have as many boyfriends as you want pretty soon, and trust me, you won't want most of them." She yawned and stood. "I'm going to bed." She kissed Frankie. "G'night, sweetie."

Alone again, Frankie looked down at her phone.

Lester? Charlotte had texted four minutes before. *You still there?*

still here, Frankie texted back. *we should try older guys*

what? why?

all the guys we know are assholes

and your point?

older ones are probs better

doubt it. how old?

seniors?

U r insane. seniors won't look at us

older then

pervy old men? great

college guys

yeah right, you gler. Anyway college guys are probs assholes too plus your mom wouldn't let you

U r so negative

so realistic u mean

Such a downer I mean

Low expectations = key to happiness

U r depressing. Gtg. Love you

Love you too

NOTHING

It's Sunday morning at Frankie's house. I slept over last night. One hundred percent honesty: I don't like sleeping at other people's houses, even Frankie's. Other people have weird stuff for breakfast and no coffee and you can't walk around in your underwear and I like my room and I hate that thing where you have to wait around for the other person to wake up because it's not your house. In a perfect world, I'd have stayed at Frankie's until three in the morning and then gone home, which by the way is what I'm planning to do if I ever have a boyfriend—in the unlikely event—because no way can I be all pretty and nice in the morning, and besides, boys aren't exactly fresh then, either.

Excuse me. Off topic.

Anyway. Even though I don't like sleepovers, I slept over at Frankie's because last night was Ollie's birthday party, which consisted of eight seventh-grade boys coming over to play video games. I repeat, eight twelve-year-old boys. Ew. Definitely time to cat. My mom was jealous.

Frankie and I are in the kitchen having pancakes, which, yum, is probably a better breakfast than I'd have at home, even though Sharon (that's Frankie's mom) makes us eat a bunch of tangerines, too. It's okay, though, because she actually peels the tangerines for us, which would never happen at my house. Frankie's parents are much more into healthy food than my parents. My mom buys cookies and chips and root beer and shit like that; she says it's because she doesn't want us eating the good food. Sharon and Tom are super-fit. They exercise a lot. Tom runs marathons—or he has, anyway. I don't know if he still does. They're really skinny. Come to think of it, this is probably why Frankie's thin and I'm not. I should start eating better.

So. The phone rings, landline, and Sharon calls from somewhere else, "Frankie, can you get that?"

Frankie sighs and gets up. "Hello?"

I hear a lot of crackling.

"Yeah. Uh-huh—ohh. *Right.*" Frankie is looking at me and

rolling her eyes. What? "Sure. Hang on." Frankie is not—sorry, Franklin, it's the truth—super-great with grown-ups. She smiles a lot, but she doesn't really *talk* to them. It's like she's embarrassed by their oldness.

"Da-aad!" she hollers. "It's Bix!"

He's in another room, too, but he comes, looking harried. He pretty much always looks that way. He's a nervous guy, Tom.

He takes the phone and listens to a lot of crackling. Frankie comes back to the table and starts arguing with me about what I just wrote.

"You are too," I say. "It's like you're embarrassed for them because they're going to die before you."

"God, I'm not even thinking about them dying! It's more like I'm worried that I'm not, uh, you know, up to expectations—that's what it is—"

"Bix! Bix! Hang on! It's—"

Crackle, crackle.

"No! No! It's fine! No!" His eyes are wide. He's freaking. "Okay. Yeah, it's totally fine. It's like you're arguing with me, but I'm not arguing. It's *fine*."

I nudge Frankie. "That's his ex? Her name's Bix?"

She nods, listening to her dad.

"Is that her real name?"

She shrugs.

"Yeah. Right. No problem. She'll be fine with it. Okay. I'll tell him. Yeah—I'll call him. Okay, fine. You call him. Okay. All right. Bye." He hangs up and leans against a cupboard with his eyes closed for a second. Then he shakes his head hard and opens his eyes. "Wow!"

"Dad?" says Frankie. "Is Bix her real name?"

He looks at her for a second like he doesn't speak English. Then he figures it out. "Oh. No. Sarah. You didn't know that? Sarah Bixby Beele."

"Why'd she go with Bix?" I ask.

He's surprised. I think Frankie doesn't ask him very many questions. "Her brother always called her that, and she liked it. Better than Sarah, anyway. So when she went to college, she told everyone her name was Bix." He smiles at me. He's handsomer than most dads. Like what you think of when you think of A Handsome Man. My dad is older than him, I'm pretty sure. "Sharon!" he calls. "Where are you, anyway?"

I nudge Frankie and whisper, "What's Bix look like?"

"Blond," she whispers. "Pink face. Tense."

Unlike Frankie, I love asking questions. I like finding stuff out about people. That's why I would've been a great spy. My parents ruined my life.

In comes Sharon. She has amazing skin. She could be in one of those Radiance at Any Age ads. She and Tom are talking, and I'm paying attention to my pancake, when Frankie says, "Wait—what?"

Her parents turn around, surprised again. It's like grown-ups think we're not listening if they're not talking to us. "Well," answers her dad. "Bix called."

"I know," says Frankie. "Remember? I answered the phone. But what about Lee?" Lee's her half-brother. He's seriously fucked up, and not in a fun way. "Is he coming for Christmas?" She sounds stressed. I would be, too.

"No," says Sharon quickly, and Frankie exhales. "No, Lee and Bix are going for a"—she glances at Tom—"cleanse in Vermont for two weeks during Christmas, and it turns out that Max wants to bring home a friend for the whole vacation and Bix is upset because she doesn't want to tell him he can't, but she doesn't want them in her house alone, so she's asking if Max and his friend can stay here for a couple weeks."

"Oh," Frankie says, relaxing against the back of her chair. "That's cool."

"Yeah, it's fine," her dad says. "But Bix has to turn everything into a conflict. Have I *ever* objected to having Max? No. Have I ever objected to Bix having Max? No! She wants to take him to Mexico for three weeks, do I say, One of those is my week? Of course not! I say, Have fun."

Speaking of people who turn things into a conflict.

Sharon is murmuring soothingly and I'm swishing my

pancake around to soak up more syrup and planning how I'm going to eat salad for lunch, when I glance up to see an extremely bizarre look on Frankie's face. "What?" I say.

She tilts her head toward her parents. "So?"

I stare at her. What is she talking about?

She wiggles her eyebrows at me.

Oh. Max and friend. College guys. Give me a break. "Loser," I say to her.

She kicks me under the table.

After breakfast, we try on about thirty outfits, and I end up in this adorable maroon striped shirt of Frankie's that I dibs if she dies (and which, since she's probably not going to die, I'm going to try keeping until she forgets about it), leggings, and my new favorite thing, Crocs and socks. I saw this friend of mine on Instagram, Jane, wear Crocs and socks together, and since she's in, like, New Zealand or something and won't ever find out, I copied.

Frankie is wearing leggings and a blue shirt that says EDGAR on it. Frankie looks better in leggings than I do. The problem is, I'm short. Mostly, I don't mind being short. In fact, I like it. But I think maybe leggings look better if you've got more leg. Just facing facts here.

It's not like I'm not pretty. I am honestly speaking pretty. I can't believe I wrote that. I have long brownish-blondish hair that's wavy and thick and nice if I use conditioner a lot. Also brown eyes, and you know what I think is the best thing about my eyes? The whites of my eyes are really super-white. It looks good. It cracks me up that no one notices this. They all say, Oh you have such beautiful eyes, but it's not the color or the shape or anything—it's the whites. My skin is not so hot. My dermatologist is Russian and a total hardass, and she's always saying that my skin would be better if I didn't wear makeup, and I'm, like, Easy for you to say, you don't have to walk around looking like a seeping wound. My mom says it'll clear up soon (actually what she says is "This too shall pass"). In the meantime, I'm wearing makeup. Mouth, good. Brows, very good—it's like nature did me this one huge favor: they're perfectly symmetrical and winged. Nose—what can I say? I like it. I like big noses. I think small noses look weird. When I was little, I felt sorry for people who had small noses, because I thought they could only take small breaths. I still kind of think that.

While we get dressed and do our makeup—Frankie just got a white eyeliner for accents, and it looks amazing—we each get about two hundred texts from people asking us what we're doing, so then we have to send two hundred texts back telling everyone we're going Christmas shopping and then another two hundred to figure out where to meet up, etcetera, etcetera, all of which makes us really late, so we don't get to the mall until almost two thirty and I'm hungry again, but I'm not going to eat anything because I can't spend money on food. I only have, like, fifty dollars, and Christmas is in two weeks! I have to buy presents for Mom and Dad and Ollie, for sure, and also for Frankie unless we decide we're not. And there's Noony and Gaby, who are super high-up on the friend scale, so I should really get them something. But if I get them something, am I leaving out poor Eden? She probably won't notice. But no matter what I do, there'll be some loaf who ruins my life by buying me a present when I haven't bought her one. Whoever she is, I hate her.

We meet up with Gaby outside Panda Express (gross!), and we're heading down to the Body Shop (Absinthe Body Butter for Mom?) when we run into

1. Soren and Devon, the guys Frankie kind of suggested were gay last week. Maybe they *are* gay. They keep slapping each other on the head. Whatever. They try to act all hard around us, saying shit like "I flexin'" and "He doin' the most." Yeah, right, whiteboy.

2. Talia, who's in French with Frankie and chem with me. She's got, like, six shopping bags full of stuff. Maybe she's rich. We say come on and hang with us, but she can't because she's with some other kids.

3. Dominic with—get this—Amelia! She's a bitch and he's

an asshole—what a perfect couple! She pretends not to notice us and is making out with him on the benches in front of Sur La Table. Good thing I didn't eat.

4. Maia H. with her mom and two little kids who are probably her brothers or sisters. She just waves.

5. A girl named Chloe I don't know but Frankie does. They hug.

6. Vlad, probably the coolest guy at Arteaga, who you hardly ever *see*, he's so famous. He's a rapper, but not in a stupid way—he's actually done videos with real artists like BTB, and Gaby says he's signed (which is cool even if it's some label in, like, Oakland, not LA). But Vlad's coolness is bigger than just rapping. He's also some kind of piano genius. At the winter concert, he played this ass-kicking thing that hardly anyone can play, which caused grown-ups to lose their shit and Channel 4 News to come and interview him, whoo-whoo. So: fame.

But. Also. Raging hot.

And—oh my god—he's walking toward me and Gaby and Frankie, and he lifts his chin at us and says, "Hey."

And we fall down dead.

No. We lift our chins and say, "Hey." So, not exactly life-changing, maybe, but we are now touched by Vlad-level cool. No more than thirty seconds after it happens, I get a text from Cora: *you're friends with Vlad?* It's so fun not answering. It says,

Sorry, I'm too busy hooking up with Vlad inside the PacSun dressing room to text you back.

7. Kellen, who's trying to find Cora but can't, so he's all, "Hey, come hang with me, Frankie!" But Frankie is now so touched by Vlad-level cool that she says, "Sorry, busy." He looks surprised. Guess no one's ever turned him down before. Get used to it, douche.

After that, we run off, giggling and snorting, and practically impale ourselves on this row of bizarre, four-foot-high plastic stockings filled with plastic presents. What the hell are they for? Frankie goes off on this thing about how they hide little bitty security guards inside, so we bang on them and then a real security guard comes and yells at us, and we go running off again, giggling and snorting some more. The mall is stuffed with gazillions of people: a million families wearing identical fuzzy Santa hats, a million little kids in stroller lockdown, a million middle-school girls buying candles and squealing at a million middle-school boys, a million old people with dogs, a million perfume-squirter ladies, a million uninterested guys selling phone cases, and a million hand-holding couples trying to figure out how much they're supposed to spend on each other for Christmas. The noise is incredible. Everyone's yelling about they want this or they want that or they don't have enough money or I told you to stay right there or I'm hungry—and on top of it all, Christmas fucking carols. I hate Christmas carols (unless it's actually Christmas or it's in church or— I'm not a *total* bitch—little kids are singing them) and the Christmas carols I hate the most are the jazzy ones they play at malls, like gross old boozy guys singing about I'll Keep You Warm on Christmas. Gag.

When we're done in the Body Shop (I don't think my mom would like Absinthe Body Butter, really) we head toward H&M (a shirt, maybe?), and we think we'll try on these cute T-shirts, but the line's too long (I don't see anything my mom would wear except a blouse, and it's twenty-eight dollars), so we give up on that and go to Francesca's (not for me, but Gaby and Frankie have sisters) and we see a bunch of kids we know there but I'm not going to write out who they are, because I already did that and I'm tired of it. Gaby finds some earrings for her sister, yay, but the line's crazy, so Frankie and I decide we'll go over to Urban while we wait. But that turns out to be depressing because the store is full of displays that say, "Party Like You Mean It!" along with these really cute party dresses and skirts, which makes it pretty clear that everyone but us is going to fabulous, exciting parties every single night. We are losers. We are knock. The last time I needed a party dress was in eighth grade, during the Bar 'n' Bat Mitzvah era. That was two years ago.

So we depressedly leave Urban and depressedly walk along

a row of little stores that are too expensive for us, and I am just depressedly texting Gaby where we are, when Frankie says, "Check that out." She nods toward a dress in the window of a store called Nostalgia.

It's a dress, a black velvet dress with a satin off-the-shoulder neckline. It's vintage and I guess it's elegant, but it's for someone old. I say, "Yeah. Cool."

"I'm going to try it on," says Frankie, and pushes open the door of Nostalgia. Of course, I follow, but I'm thinking, This is pointless, you can't get it anyway. I mean, first of all, it's black and wearing all-black is emo. Rawr XD. You get a lot of shit if you wear all-black (unless you're Priya Lo or something). Second of all, as I just finished saying, the last time we needed party dresses was two years ago, and even if we did get invited to a party, it wouldn't be the kind of party you could wear this dress to. This is a cocktail party–type dress. Third, it is definitely out of our price range. And fourth: it's a dress for, like, a woman, not a kid. It's outside the boundaries of our context, just like Ms. Heath (that's my English teacher) says about everything. So why bother?

But Frankie, after, amazingly, speaking to the saleslady (who must buy foundation in gallon jars) goes into a dressing room with the black dress, so I stand by, watching the saleslady's face. I wonder if she has to reapply during the day. Maybe she just re-powders. Then I wonder how stores like this stay in business. The mall is total madness, stuffed with shoppers—and in here, there's just me and Frankie. And it's not like we're going to buy anything.

Frankie flings open the curtain and I squeak. Honestly, I squeak. Because she looks unbelievable. I can't even describe it. She looks like she's maybe twenty, and if her hair were up, she'd look older. She also looks amazing. Glamorous. Nobody our age looks glamorous. She looks like she has ten parties to go to, and she'll see if she can fit them all in. She looks like a model. She looks like what my dad would call a knockout.

"I know," Frankie says. She turns to look at herself in the mirror. "I look old."

"You look incredible."

She doesn't bother to deny it. She just keeps on looking at herself with this funny expression on her face. She's not posing or fake-modeling, the way I'd probably be doing if I was wearing a dress that made me look like that. I wonder what she's thinking, and I'm about to ask her when the saleslady comes to look.

"My," she says. "That's definitely your dress, isn't it?" But she knows we're not buying, so she goes away.

"How much is it?" Frankie whispers, trying to reach the tag on the back.

"A hundred and fifty-five." Whew.

She nods. "Take a picture of me."

I do.

"Send it to me."

I do.

We look at her some more, and then she sort of sighs and goes back in the dressing room. "Gimme your phone," I call while I wait for her to get dressed.

"Why?"

"Shut up and give it to me," I say. So she hands it out. And in about twenty seconds, the picture is flying through air molecules toward Frankie's mom with the message: Frankie wants this for Christmas. Plus where it is, and even how much it costs.

I am Santa's elf.

After something like twenty texts, we figure out where Gaby is, which is—oh little fucking town of Bethlehem—still in Francesca's. There are about fifty people squashed in there, so Frankie and I wait outside, but outside is directly under a speaker, so it's like we're being hosed with Christmas carols.

"If they don't stop playing that song, I'm going to scream," I mutter.

Frankie starts up, "Ding-dinga-ding, ding-dinga-ding, hey it's lovely weather for a sleigh ride together with *yoooouuu*."

I scream.

Gaby sticks her head out of Francesca's. "What happened?"

"Char's screaming because she loves Christmas so much," says Frankie, but here comes that same dang security guard again, and I guess you're not supposed to scream at the mall—although, I have to say, under the circumstances, screaming seems pretty reasonable. Anyway, we cat and meet Gaby a few minutes later at the Alamo, which is the piercing place and the only really cool store in the entire mall. We wander around, looking at studs and rings and gages, and Gaby wants her nose pierced, bad.

"Should I just do it?" she asks. "My mom'll kill me if I do."

"Same with my mom," says Frankie. "Even a tiny stud will cause instant death."

My mom says that if I want to have my boogers come flying out the side of my nostril when I sneeze, it's okay with her, but this is one of those things I don't mention to Gaby and Frankie. Instead, I say, "I know! For Christmas, you guys could give your mom the gift of not getting your nose pierced. Like, write it on a card, and that's the present!"

"Nice!" says Gaby.

"Well, it's what she wants, right?" I say.

"Hell, yeah!" says Frankie. "I'm doing it. Total savings of probably twenty-five dollars I would have spent on her. You're a genius, Char."

Gaby looks at her phone and has a seasonal freak-out. "Oh my god, it's five! Come on, you guys. We have to get serious about this."

We get serious, and I am now broke.

God Forbid You Should Actually Learn Something

Almost. Almost. The last day of school before Christmas vacation moved like mud. Frankie's geometry class alone had lasted twenty years. Even lunch break went on too long— all the kids who had gotten wasted in the bathroom were screaming and throwing their Secret Santa candy canes at each other, and all the kids who hadn't were opening gift bags and hugging each other. And then it went limp; everyone was tired and screamed out, and there was a lot of too-loud laughter about stupid jokes. Frankie was secretly glad when the bell rung.

Well, maybe not *glad*, Frankie thought. Glad would be

going too far. She locked her jaw against a yawn and looked at Miss Mathers's clock for approximately the twentieth time since the class had begun. 2:37. Oh my god. Thirty-three more minutes.

Miss Mathers was definitely not the type to have a Christmas party on the last day before vacation. Oh no, Miss Mathers was the type to torture them by having what she called a "Literary Round Table" instead. That's where everyone—*everyone!*—had to say something they found "thought-provoking" in the book they were supposed to be reading, *The Free Throw Line*. Which in addition to being amazingly hard to say, was also the most depressing book in the history of the world. English-class books were always pretty bad, but this was worse than usual: poor Mexican kid named Javier tries to cross the US border but gets caught and sent to a camp/prison, where his incredible basketball skills are seen by a guard who adopts him to cash in on his talent. He becomes a basketball star! Except then his dad back home gets killed by drug dealers, and Javier returns to Mexico to help his mom, but the only job he can find is working for the cartel as a runner. One day during a drop, Javier by mistake kills his best friend—the guy who taught him how to play basketball in the first place—goes crazy, shoots himself in the hand, and can never play basketball again. The end.

Frankie, one of the six or seven kids in the class who'd

actually done the reading, had contributed her thought-provokement right at the beginning of the Round Table, to get it over with, but she was regretting it now, as she listened to person after person say, "I really liked the part where he, uh—you know—like when he was playing ball and, uh, made the free throw [because they figured that the guy had to have made a free throw at least once for the book to be called *The Free Throw Line*]. That part was really thought-provoking."

Then Miss Mathers would say, "What did you find thought-provoking about it?"

And Kid X would look at her blankly and say, "The free throw."

Help me, God, prayed Frankie. Send earthquake. Now!

She looked at the clock again. 2:44. Twenty-six more minutes.

"I must say, I am very disappointed in the quality of your work, students," sniffed Miss Mathers. She whirled around on OCD Luis. "Luis, let's hear what you have to say."

Frankie stiffened with pity. Poor Luis. He could barely talk when someone spoke to him nicely, and Miss Mathers's whirling and sniffing was going to freak him out.

It did.

Luis began stuttering, "Uh, uh—okay, uh—well—uh—"

And one of the asshole Chrises yelled, "Spit it out, Louie!"

"Chris! That's enough!" snapped Miss Mathers.

"What? *What?* I was just, like, trying to help!"

Sweating, Luis tried again. "I—I—was—well—"

"Have you *done* the reading, Luis?" snapped Miss Mathers. You bitch, thought Frankie. Of course he's done it.

"Yes!" cried Luis, shaking now. "Yes!"

"Because I'm afraid I'm not seeing much evidence of that. If you had read it, you would surely have found something to say about it."

"I read it!" Luis panted. "I read it, and—" He broke off.

"Yes?" said Miss Mathers nastily.

"Why doesn't anything good ever happen to Mexicans in books?" he said in a rush. "That's what I thought. Why are Mexicans always so, like, down and messed up? Like, is there some law that Mexicans can't have good lives?"

There was a brief, shocked pause. No one had ever heard Luis say that many words before.

Then one of the Chrises said, "Try the black man, Louie. They worse."

And the other Chris said, "That's racist, man."

"Shut up. I'm black. I can't be racist," said Chris. Then to Luis. "You ever seen an okay—like, normal—black guy in a book? Shit you have. They're always fu—"—he glanced at Miss Mathers—"messed up."

Race. Oh my god, *race.* The classroom was frozen with panic.

Except Luis, who said in a shaky voice, "It's depressing. Why can't we read something about someone Mexican who's, like, happy?"

Then Raven spoke up. Raven Nuts, who had a shaved head and talked to herself and who everyone avoided because she was just too scary—*that* Raven—said, "It's a control technique. They give us these books so we'll think the world is so terrifying that we can never hope to succeed in it unless we follow their rules and behave ourselves. If we're happy, we're out of their control."

Which was so unbelievably like what Frankie had always felt but had never been able to put into words that she found herself saying, "Yeah!"

"But that's mean," Luis objected.

Raven shrugged. "And this surprises you?"

Chris started laughing.

Miss Mathers broke in. "Why, that's just silly, Raven! We read to *learn* about the experiences of other people." She looked around the room, smiling nervously. "We are on a tangent, boys and girls. Let's return to our Round Table discussion—"

Frankie looked at the clock. 2:57.

And. And. And . . .

3:10! The bell rang, and a survivors' cheer went up all over the school. In Miss Mathers's class, the thunder of thirty-one kids un-wedging themselves from desks, squishing binders into backpacks, putting on jackets, and pulling out phones was even more thunderous than usual. As her students stampeded out of her classroom, Miss Mathers stood stiffly by her desk, flicking papers around, a tiny, tense smile on her face. Frankie surprised herself by feeling sorry for her.

"Have a good one, Miss Mathers," called unnaturally polite Josh.

"Thank you, Josh," she said primly. "Same to you." Having been relieved of the burden of being so disliked as to receive not a single good-bye, her shoulders relaxed.

So did Frankie's. Thank you, unnaturally polite Josh. She smiled at him, and he smiled back. "Have a good one, Frankie," he said brightly.

Did you go to military school or something? she thought. "You too, Josh."

Breaking a path through the teeming corridors toward her locker, Frankie caught a glimpse of Raven hoisting her bulging black backpack onto her shoulder. In addition to the bulging black backpack, she carried a small ice chest—the kind that usually held a six-pack—with a biohazard sticker on it and a French horn case.

"Hey Raven," Frankie called, surprising herself again. "That was good, what you said."

The backpack fell off Raven's shoulder and she dropped

the ice chest. "Thanks," she said, re-slinging the backpack.

Frankie picked up the ice chest and handed it to her. "I thought that, too, kind of, but I could never think how to say it."

Raven took the ice chest and nodded. "Cool. Thanks." She didn't seem to have anything to add.

Frankie realized that she'd thought Raven would be glad—maybe even sort of honored—that Frankie was talking to her, since most people didn't. But Raven wasn't. Embarrassed, Frankie looked down at the ice chest. "Is there really a biohazard in there?

Raven tilted her head and looked at Frankie sideways. "Plague bacillus."

Frankie took a step back.

Raven laughed. "No. It's my lunch, really."

"Weirdo," Frankie said.

Raven snickered and turned to go. "See ya."

"Have a good one."

"Yeah," said Raven. "Don't let 'em shit on your dreams."

"Lottie! Baby!" Frankie hollered.

Charlotte pulled her eyes away from her phone. "Lester, baby," she said, but her voice was muted.

"What?" Frankie hurried over. "What's up?"

"He's just so—great." Charlotte sighed. She held out her phone. "Look."

Frankie didn't need to ask who she was talking about. Sid. She looked. It was a photo of a snowman, only it wasn't a snowman, it was just a face, sculpted in snow. But it was an artwork, too, because the face looked almost alive. The way it was smiling, with one-half of its mouth higher than the other half—it looked like it had just stopped laughing.

"Wow. Did he make that?" asked Frankie.

"Yeah. I think," said Charlotte. "See what he says?"

Like my selfie? read Frankie. "That's him?" she asked, even though she knew Charlotte didn't know. There were no pictures of Sid. Not anywhere. He didn't allow it, and he wouldn't say why. All he said was that he wanted to be hard to find when they came looking for him—which Charlotte thought was a joke, but Frankie wasn't so sure. Charlotte had met Sid on Instagram through a friend of her cousin, and they texted all the time, but they'd never met in real life, and Charlotte was positive they never would because he lived a state away, in Oregon. Frankie had pointed out that a state away wasn't an insurmountable obstacle. It wasn't like he lived in the Himalayas, for instance. And Charlotte said Sisters, Oregon, *was* like the Himalayas if you were fifteen. Frankie said that was a defeatist attitude, and then Charlotte got pissed off and said she didn't care what Frankie thought, she wasn't going to waste emotional energy hoping to meet a guy she was never going to meet who probably didn't give a shit about her anyway, which was when Frankie realized that Charlotte really, really liked him.

Not that she would ever admit it.

It made Frankie crazy, the way Charlotte refused to get excited about anything, like she had a policy against it, but Frankie had known her for a long time, and she knew that Charlotte did care about stuff, a lot. She was just scared to say so. It was like she'd made a bargain with the devil or something, that as long as she didn't say she wanted anything—like, for instance, meeting Sid—her life wouldn't be ruined. But if she ever dared to admit, out loud, that she was hoping for thing X to happen, she would be destroyed. Frankie didn't really get it. Obviously, no one likes to be embarrassed, but why would Charlotte's life be more ruined if she admitted she was into Sid and it turned out he wasn't into her than it would be if she didn't admit it (but still was) and he wasn't into her?

Privately Frankie thought Sid's no-picture policy was weird, but Charlotte thought it made him intriguing and different. And even Frankie had to agree that his Instagram was pretty cool. He was a great photographer, and he didn't take pictures of the usual stuff—sunsets, flowers, pretty people. He took pictures of things you mostly didn't notice. He'd done a whole series on the backs of people's heads, which had made Frankie really look at the backs of people's heads for the first time. There was a lot of personality in head backs.

"How would I know if it's him?" Charlotte said. She leaned over Frankie's shoulder and looked at the snow face. "Isn't it good, though? See how he did the smile?"

"Yeah. He's good," said Frankie.

Charlotte rubbed her chin against Frankie's shoulder. "*Maybe* he's good. If it's him who made it. Maybe his girlfriend made it."

"Oh, right!" Frankie slapped her forehead. "I forgot about her! His long-legged, big-boobed girlfriend with perfect eyebrows! Who's also incredibly talented! She must've made it!"

"And after she was done," Charlotte continued, "they ripped off all their clothes—"

"And had sex—"

"In the snow," added Charlotte. She was giggling now.

"But!" Frankie held up a finger. "They didn't feel the cold, because . . ."

"They're so fucking hot!" yelled Charlotte.

Frankie put her arms around Charlotte and squeezed. "Not that you care."

Charlotte burrowed her face into Frankie's jacket, and for a second, she was quiet. "I don't even know the guy. We text all the time, but I know nothing about him. Except what he decides to tell me."

Frankie nodded.

"I know—I mean, I'm sure—that it wouldn't turn into anything. But still, it would be nice to—you know, meet him. Not that I will."

"Maybe you will," said Frankie. "It's possible."

"Oh yeah," said Charlotte, pulling her face out of Frankie's jacket to give her a don't-be-a-moron look. "Next time I'm passing through Sisters, Oregon, I'll drop in."

"Well," said Frankie, a little defensively, "it could happen. You could make it happen."

Charlotte shook her head. "By the time I could make it happen, I won't care."

"Don't let 'em shit on your dreams," said Frankie.

"What?"

Frankie hesitated. "I mean, don't just—surrender. It's like you give up without even trying sometimes. I think you should, well, aim for more. You know." She made a fist. "You gotta fight the fight."

Charlotte glared at her. "You gotta shut the mouth."

Frankie sighed. "You are such a twat." She gathered Charlotte into her arms and gave her one more squeeze. "Come on!" She lifted Charlotte off the ground. "Let's get this Christmas break rolling!"

NOTHING

Frankie and Gaby and Noony and I solved our Christmas-present dilemma by giving each other mascara. On the Saturday after the Friday we got out for break, we went to CVS and bought it together, which was really fun and also didn't cost that much (even though Noony wanted this fancy kind that cost fifteen dollars. Frankie and I went together on it). Afterward, we were walking up Redwood Road, looking in the stores, when we passed the drug addict Christmas tree lot and saw this pathetic little tree that nobody would ever buy in a million years. We were joking around about how it made us want to cry, and I ran in and asked if we could have it for two dollars, and the guy gave it to me for free! Then we went back to CVS and all chipped in to buy some cheapo gold balls. We went up to Canyon Rock and stuck the little tree in a crack and decorated it. It turned out to be really pretty up there, with the sun setting and the gold balls all sparkly. We got high and Noony started singing "The Twelve Days of Christmas," and these hipsters joined in, and then we were all singing it, and it was fun, even though we only got up to the tenth day and we were too lazy to look up what came next. We took a bunch of pictures, and then Alex and Reed and this friend of Reed's named Arian showed up. We got cold after a while and went down to my house and ate ramen and Oreos.

It was pretty normal but at the same time, pretty nice, too.

So I was happy.

And then Frankie went psycho.

Okay, maybe not medical-grade psycho, but definitely off. She's been off all break. It began on the Friday school got out, when she was ragging on me about Sid—you don't try hard enough, you've got to fight the fight (what fight?), you've got to make it happen. Which is sort of mean, in my opinion, because it's like accusing me of lack of effort, when really, there's no effort I can make that will result in me meeting the guy. Okay? So it's like she's saying I'm a pussy. And then I start wondering, am I a pussy? Am I, like, defective? Would someone else be able to figure out how to make it happen? I worry about this.

That was the beginning.

Then, on Sunday, Silent Max comes home with his friend Grant.

And Frankie loses her shit.

Get this: Grant sleeps all day. He gets up at, like, five in the afternoon, eats dinner, and then he and Max go out to—what?—clubs, I guess, until three or four in the morning. And then he sleeps all the next day, repeat, repeat.

To me, this seems like normal college-guy behavior.

But oh my fucking god, Frankie thinks he's got some mysterious condition, I can't remember the name of it, like a sun allergy. People who have it can't go outside during the day and they're called, according to Frankie, Children of the Night.

The internet, where logic goes to die.

Frankie gets all obsessed, and for two days she calls me every time she has a Grant sighting, to tell me how pale he is, and all about his potentially pathetic life expectancy and oh my god low sperm count, and I keep saying, "Wow!" and "Huh!" and "Poor guy!" because I want to be a supportive friend, but inside I'm thinking: *You are a fucking loon.*

And on day three, she Facetimes me at ten a.m., which is a little bit on the early side for Christmas vacation, so my mouth is full of toast when I accept. "Wha?"

"He doesn't have it," she whispers.

I have no idea what she's talking about so I say "Wha?" again.

"Grant. He and Max are going to the beach today."

I swallow. "Ohhh. No Child of the Night, then."

"Right."

I don't know what a supportive friend is supposed to say here, so I say, "That's good."

She makes a feh noise. "He's also really short."

"Well. At least he's got plenty of sperm."

Thank god, she busts up laughing. But after we shit-talk Grant for a while, she says, "I gotta go."

"'Kay. How come?"

"I'm going on a thing."

"What thing?"

She hesitates—she'd make a crap spy—and says, "It's just this thing."

"Franklin."

"Okay, okay." She sighs, and then she says quick, "I'm going on a tour of St. Albans."

"*What?*" St. Albans is St. Albans College Preparatory. It's a fancy private school for assholes that's over in Coso, which is about forty minutes away. "What the fuck are you talking about?"

"I'm just taking the tour, Char. It's nothing. I'll probably hate it."

"*Why* are you taking the tour? You don't even like school—why would you want to go to fucking college prep? Those kids have six hours of homework a night." Not to mention it costs, like, thirty thousand a year.

She starts hemming and hawing. "It's just my dad. He wanted me to take a look."

This is total bullshit, because her dad always wanted her to take a look, and Frankie always said no. "Frankie! Who do you think you're talking to here? Are you really thinking about going there? Why didn't you tell me? What the hell is going on?"

"It's just a tour, Char," she says in this kind of weary voice. "I just want to see if—maybe it would be good to do something different, you know?"

"I can't believe you didn't say anything to me." My feelings are hurt, I admit it.

"It's just a tour," she says again. Then her mom comes in the room. "I gotta slide, Char."

I don't even say good-bye. I just hang up.

And of course, she does hate it. Duh. About two hours later, I get a text: *Help! I'm surrounded by assholes*

My feelings are still hurt, so I don't answer. About two minutes later, I get another one: *omg they're talking about how much they love studying until 3am*

I don't answer.

Two minutes later: *this ho is saying how college was easy next to StA*

I don't answer.

Two minutes later: *now this other ho is saying StA gives her life*
purpose

    I relent: Jay Alvarrez gives my life purpose

    Now everyone's looking at me cause I'm laughing

    No laughing allowed

    I hate this place

    Good I'm still mad though

    I love u, Char

So I stop being mad because—well, because it's Christmastime, and I am filled with peace and love and goodwill toward men, including Frankie. But I am watching, too, because I'm not an idiot, and I know what it means that Frankie's gone batshit, that she's obsessing about stupid Grant and touring St. Albans School for Assholes. It means she wants something to change—she wants to jump off the ledge—and that means that I'm probably going to be out of a best friend pretty soon. Because Frankie's not getting change on the earthshaking life-or-death level, and not on the love-n-sex level either. The school level was a bust. That leaves the friend level. So I'm trying to get ready. Does that sound cynical and heartless? Too bad. I'm being realistic here. You know, practical. Protected is another way to say it, I guess.

* * *

Christmas. I hope I never get over Christmas. I remember when I was a little kid, and Christmas Eve was the most exciting thing in the world. Ollie and I would sleep in the same room, and we'd promise to wake each other up at three a.m. to catch Santa Claus coming down the chimney. I don't know why we thought three a.m. was the right time, but we did. Or I did, and Ollie believed me. He was so cute back then; he frowned all the time. Everything you said to him, he frowned and nodded, like a doctor. We never woke up at three a.m., but it was fun planning it. And then, oh my god, the total died-and-went-to-heaven of Christmas morning, coming downstairs and seeing a field of presents under the tree. Even if a lot of them were for cousins and shit, it was beautiful.

It's not like that anymore. I mean, it's not really exciting the way it used to be, since I know that most of my presents are going to be gift cards, plus Mom's annual experiment in teen fashion (every year, she wings it on one gift, because she thinks gift cards are lame. She does okay. Not perfect, but okay, as in, I usually don't have to return it). But Christmas is still good—I mean, I like gift cards, and I still get a little flash of the old died-and-went-to-heaven feeling on Christmas morning. I hope I keep it forever, and even if I can't, I hope I don't turn into one of those grown-ups who mutters bitterly about how much trouble Christmas is.

We did our traditional Christmas things—my aunt Louise and her new husband (I think I should be calling him my uncle) came for a few days; we went to my granddad's for Christmas Eve and had cioppino (and Granddad let me have a glass of wine!); we opened presents on Christmas morning with the cousin assortment pack; and we went to my dad's younger brother Sam's house for Christmas dinner, which was goose, yuck, but my aunt Vaughn (who's a girl, even though her name is Vaughn) made the most delicious mocha torte you ever tasted in your life. She's a pastry chef for a caterer, and boy, are we glad Sam married her.

Impressive semicolon use in that paragraph.

I got a bunch of good stuff, too—cards for iTunes, H&M, and PacSun. Mom's present was a sweater from Brandy, which isn't what I'd normally wear but might be okay, plus it was nice of her because she hates Brandy. Ollie and I got each other the same thing: iTunes cards (but the one I gave him was for more than the one he gave me. Which is fine). Dad did what he always does, which is wait until the twenty-third and then freak out, so he got me watercolor paints and paper, which is kind of goofy, but fun. And Louise, who must really be happy about that new husband (Uncle Marshall) gave me seventy-five dollars!

So Christmas was nice, just like it always is, and afterward, on Christmas night, I got kind of blue, just like I always do. When I was little, Christmas night was a full-on spiral into despair, but now, I just get a little blue. So I wandered around my room for a while and I tried on my new sweater and—see how incredibly honest I'm being in this book?—I played with these little wooden mice I've had since I was tiny. Then my phone buzzes. Frankie!

Frankie Radiates Positive Energy and Nobody Dies as a Result

"Hey," said Frankie. She wedged the phone between her pillow and her ear. "You're the best, you know that?"

"You mean the dress?" asked Charlotte. "Merry Christmas, by the way. You didn't even guess, did you?"

"No! No idea. I couldn't believe it when I opened the box."

"So did you wear it?" Charlotte asked. "Like for dinner or something? You guys do a fancy Christmas dinner, don't you?"

Frankie made a bitter noise. "Fancy, right. Max and Grant were rocking sweatpants, and Cate was wearing six tank tops—I have no idea why she does that. I want to say, Put on a fucking sweater, you gler. But then she'd stab me."

"Put the steak knife down, Cate."

Frankie giggled. "And my poor dad—this is so completely sad—my mom's mom gave him one of those aprons with the picture of a super-ripped guy's body on it, you know, naked except for bulging undies."

"Oh my god."

"Yeah, she said she thought he'd like it because he's so into exercise. A *little* bit passive-aggressive, maybe?"

"Just a little. Jesus."

"And since Grandma was right there, he had to wear it while he cooked. Every time he looked down, he turned red."

"Poor Tom. But Cate must've been happy, watching him get embarrassed."

"Oh so happy. Best Christmas she ever had. She was so happy she even helped clean up, which made my mom feel good. So that was okay, but I'm kind of glad it's over."

"It's not over." Charlotte yawned. "We have thirteen more days off. That's almost two weeks."

"That's almost half a month," said Frankie. "Anything could happen."

"Want to bet?" Charlotte yawned again. "Hey, should we go shopping tomorrow afternoon? I got gift cards."

"Maybe. I might be doing something else then," said Frankie evasively. "I'll text you."

The next morning, Frankie paused outside the kitchen to take a deep breath. Nothing was going to happen if she didn't make it happen. Right? Right. A person had to *ask* for what she wanted. Right? Right. Frankie channeled positive energy and marched briskly into the kitchen, where Max was hunched over his computer, eating Rice Krispies.

"Hi!" she said, radiating positive energy.

Max lifted his eyes from his computer to Frankie.

She pulled out imaginary earbuds. He pulled out his earbuds. "What?"

"Hi," she repeated enthusiastically.

He raised his eyebrows, waiting.

"Whatcha doing?" she asked.

He cleared his throat. "I used to be watching *Fullmetal Alchemist*."

He wasn't really irritated, Frankie knew. It took a lot to irritate him. "I meant, what are you doing *today*," she said. "Like, later."

"Frankie," he said. "What do you *want*?"

"You know how you gave me a gift certificate for driving lessons for Christmas?" she said in a rush.

He nodded reluctantly.

"So? Could we go out today? Just for, like, an hour—or maybe more?" She nodded hopefully at him.

Max smiled at her. He had gotten a lot better-looking in the last year, Frankie noticed. He had been a scrawny twig guy in high school, but now he was bigger. He didn't look like a kid anymore. His hair had gotten better, too. He'd let it grow, and it had turned out to be curly.

"Okay," he said simply.

"Really?" Frankie's voice pitched upward. She hadn't expected him to say yes—knowing as she did that he'd only given her the certificate because it didn't cost anything.

"Yeah. Later. Like—" He looked at the clock. "Like, maybe, two?"

"Yess!" Frankie boinged up and down on her toes. "Two's great! Two's fantastic!"

He frowned. "You've got the permit, right?"

"Yeah, yeah, I've got the permit, I know all the rules," she assured him. "I went out with Dad a couple times, but you know, he's kind of a freak about it, and Mom won't go. She says teaching Cate traumatized her."

Max snorted. "I can see that."

Frankie giggled. "Me too. You'd crash the car just to end it."

He laughed, and Frankie felt a little rush of happiness that he thought she was funny. "Okay!" She slapped her hands together. "Two!"

He nodded and returned to his screen, reaching for his

earbuds. As he wedged one into his ear, he noticed that Frankie was still looking at him. "What?" He sighed.

"Max?"

"Yes, Frankie?"

"Do you have a girlfriend?"

He hesitated ever so slightly. "Yes."

"You do?" Frankie leaned forward, fascinated. "Really? Since when?"

"Since about two months ago." He blushed a little.

"Wow! Does she live around here?"

"No."

Frankie rubbed her fingers on the counter, filled with questions that wouldn't tell her what she wanted to know. "Do you really like her?" she said, cutting to the chase.

"No. I really hate her. Shut up."

Frankie retreated to the conventional. "What's her name?"

"Raina."

Frankie couldn't think of anything to say about that. "Huh." Pause. "Does Grant know her?"

"Yeah."

"Can I see a picture of her?"

He shook his head. "No. Could you please go away now?"

Oops. He was getting irritated. Better retreat. Frankie said, "Okay! Bye! Don't forget! Two!"

Max grunted and stuffed the other earbud in.

Back in the safety of the dining room, Frankie leaned against the wall and took out her phone to text Charlotte:

Max is taking me driving!

Yay Max! When?

Today! 2

Wait—thought it had to be someone over 25

Shutup

I'm calling the cops

FU

Look Twice Save a Life

I will!

Come over later

K. 4?

K

Frankie collapsed against the back of the driver's seat, exhausted. "When does it stop taking all your concentration?"

"It *always* takes concentration," said Max in a grown-uppy voice. He looked over at her and added, in a more friendly way, "But it gets a lot easier after the first six months."

"Good." Frankie closed her eyes. After five minutes in the car with Max, Frankie had realized that her dad didn't really want her to learn how to drive. When her dad took her out driving, they went to an empty business park and drove around an empty parking lot for about ten minutes. Max, on the other hand, had taken her down to Shellmound, which was a wide, gravelly park by the bay. There was no actual traffic, but there were other cars, as well as lanes and fences and dogs and even some people on the bicycle path, which was of course far far away from where Frankie was driving but which she could conceivably lose her mind, hit the accelerator, and careen into, killing everyone, if she didn't pay close attention. And Max, unlike her dad, kept making her try new things, like reversing, which was terrifying because you had to look in the mirror while at the same time not forgetting to look out the front window, too.

Frankie was drenched in sweat.

"You done?" asked Max.

She nodded.

"Okay, put it into Park and turn off the engine."

Frankie looked down at the gears.

"Foot on brake. Move into Park."

She put her foot on the brake and shifted into Park.

"Key."

Hesitantly, she turned the key. The car didn't leap violently forward and kill two pedestrians walking their dogs at the edge of the park. It just went off. Frankie exhaled with relief.

"You did great," said Max.

"Thanks."

There was a pause.

"So," he said. "You can get out now."

"Nuh-uh," Frankie said. "I can't unwrap my fingers from the steering wheel yet."

He laughed. "Okay. We can just sit here for a minute."

She nodded. There was a silence, and then she said, "Am I reminding you of Dad?"

"What? 'Cause you're so tense? A little."

"Fuck."

"It's okay," said Max. "Dad's okay."

There was another silence. "I always thought I was a really easygoing, chill kind of person, but I don't think I am," she said.

Max shrugged. "You're okay."

"*You're* chill," she said accusingly.

"Yeah, that's what everyone says." He grimaced. "But you know what? I hate that word. Chill. It makes me sound like those guys who think the whole point of life is playing beer pong and kicking back."

"I just meant you're calm."

"I know, I know, but it still bugs me, because whenever you want to do stuff, people act like it's some kind of personality disorder."

"I take it back. You're not chill!" Frankie thought a minute. "But I think it's good, wanting to get stuff done. You've got to, right?"

He gave her a questioning look.

"Char and I are always talking—arguing, really—about this. She thinks it's ridiculous to try to make things happen at our age. But I think you've got to at least *want* something. If you don't, you're letting yourself be crushed by other people's rules, you know?"

"Well," he said slowly, "it depends on what you want. I mean, if you want something deranged, like to be a serial killer, then yeah, you should be crushed by other people's rules."

Frankie giggled. "Well, duh. But let's say you're just, like, regular. Then I think it's okay to want your life to change, and to try to get what you want. Char thinks we should just accept that we have no power to do anything."

"Dark worldview," commented Max.

"Yeah. I think it's the books she reads."

Max smiled. "She should watch more cat videos."

Frankie unsnapped her seat belt. "Did you ever do anything completely against the rules and crazy just because you wanted to?"

"Yeah," said Max, opening his door, "I took you out driving."

"Can we go again? Like maybe tomorrow? Please?"

He turned to look at her. "You're not chill. But okay. Tomorrow."

NOTHING

In order to talk about what happened next I have to go back and explain a little—I guess this is where second drafts come in if you're a real writer, but fuck that, too boring. Okay: on Christmas Eve day, when my mom and I were making another batch of shortbread because Dad and Ollie are under the impression that if you leave one cookie in the tin, you haven't eaten all the cookies, so all of our tins had one cookie in them, I got a text from Sid: *what's your snail mail?*

I send it to him, plus: *why?*

You'll see

All through Christmas, I was wondering what he was

sending me. I mean, I wasn't freaking or anything—I was in holiday mode, jingle bells, fa la la—but in the back of my mind, I was thinking about it, off and on. The next day, too. And then the day after that, when I checked the mailbox— casually!—there was an envelope. From Sid Havelka, 17167 Foothill View Rd, Sisters, OR 97759. His handwriting is typical boy writing, blocky and dorky, like a second-grader did it. Blue pen. I keep staring and staring at his writing on the envelope, trying to figure out what he's like from his writing, which is, I guess, what you do when you have zero real facts about a person. I wish I knew what he looks like—I mean, what the fuck's with the no-picture rule? It makes you think he probably has some major disfiguring thing on his face, like two noses or one eye. But that's probably not the thing. Probably he just has acne. Well, fuck him, I have zits and I put my picture out there—why should he be so delicate?

Excuse me. Digression.

Except I really am having these thoughts while I'm staring at his envelope, being all fascinated by his blue, blocky handwriting and then getting mad at myself for being fascinated, because it's such bullshit. I mean, how manipulative is that, refusing to reveal your image so that your friends sit around wondering if you have two noses? Really manipulative. Asshole.

So I'm kind of mad and distracted by being mad when I pull open the envelope and this tiny, heavy piece of paper slides into my hand. It's a porcupine. A tiny, perfect drawing of a porcupine. I guess it's colored pencil. It's adorable. The porcupine has this annoyed look, like he was in the middle of important porcupine business and got interrupted. I turn it over and there's a message in spindly black ink: "Charlotte MC —S."

MC must be Merry Christmas.

He made me a porcupine.

I love it.

And the other thing is—he remembered. Back when we first started texting, like, last summer, he put a picture of this ugly-ass newt up on his Instagram, and I was teasing him about it, telling him there had to be better-looking animals than that, even in Sisters, Oregon. He said there weren't. I said what about hedgehogs, and he said there aren't any hedgehogs in Oregon, I must be thinking of porcupines. I said of course there are hedgehogs, and then I looked it up and he was right. There are no hedgehogs. There are porcupines.

So he made me a porcupine.

Oh my god, I am completely in love with this guy.

No I'm not. That's stupid. I don't even know him and he's manipulative as fuck. Plus, he's got acne. At best. At worst, two noses. Actually, I can think of lots of worse things than that.

Like, he's a forty-year-old child molester.

But he's not. He's in high school. I know this because the friend of a friend on Instagram, which is how I met him, actually goes to school with him. Sid's got pictures of this friend, Sukey, and a bunch of other kids, on his Instagram. Sukey lives in Sisters. My cousin Campbell knows Sukey because they worked at the same movie theater before Sukey moved. So. Sid's a child. He could still be a molester, though.

But he made me a porcupine.

I text him. It takes me a really long time.

Best present ever. I love him. 1000000 x cuter than a newt. You're amazing.

Is that okay? I don't know. Should I have said Thanks or Thank you? I tried it, but it looked weird. Like, cold and formal. Like I was writing a Thank You Note. Which, duh, was exactly what I was doing, but I didn't want to sound cold and formal.

Normally, I'd consult with Frankie about something like this. Normally, I'd have texted her about twenty seconds after I opened my porcupine and she would have come over and we would have freaked out together.

But I don't. I don't text her partly because I don't want to hear about what a pussy I am and how I have to fight the fight, but partly because if Frankie's about to break up with me, I have to have something that's just mine, a secret, a thing that won't be changed by her not being my friend anymore.

So even if she's hanging with, like, Merle and that girl Chloe, I'll still have something. I'm getting ready, just in case. So shoot me.

Frankie got her fabulous black dress for Christmas—thank you, Charlotte, for being such an outstanding friend. You're welcome. But fuck me if that dress didn't turn into the next act in the Frankie Goes Psycho show.

Right after I got my present from Sid, while I am still sort of breathtaken, Frankie calls on our landline, of all things. "Let's have a soiree!" she yells.

And because I have taken four years of French and know that soiree means fancy party (actually, it means evening-ie), I say, "Sure, Frankie, I'll be right over."

"No! Not now!" she says. "On New Year's! Let's have a really elegant dinner party and get all dressed up so I can wear my new dress. We can have Noony and Gaby and Alex and maybe Reed if we can stand him. We'll all look really smooth and we'll take a bunch of pictures and it'll be fun!"

And it does sound pretty fun. Maybe a little dorky, but fun, because New Year's Eve is usually a drag, with lots of calling around to see if anyone's having a party, which nobody ever is, and then rumors about all the really cool parties we're not invited to, followed by sulking in front of the TV at someone's house and splitting, like, nine beers between seven people.

We are bored out of our minds. A fancy dinner party at least sounds different.

Frankie says, "But we should do it at your house."

"Why?" I say, thinking of cooking and dishes and cleaning.

"Because Max and Grant are here."

That's a pretty good reason. So I say, "Okay, let me ask my mom." We hang up and I go running around the house to find my mom. Finally she turns up in her closet, trying on black T-shirts, and I tell her all about Frankie's good idea, but I make it sound like my idea. I don't want her to think Frankie's passing the buck.

"It'll be a soiree," I say. "So people will be on their best behavior and we'll clean everything up afterward. You won't have to do a thing."

She pops her head out of a T-shirt. "It would be okay, except for one problem—Daddy and I are going away that night. Don't you remember this whole thing? We're going up to Robin and Jim's beach cabin until the second, and you and Ollie are going to Granddad's. Remember?" She squints at me. "I told you about this two weeks ago."

Now, the honest answer would be: I have no recollection of it because I don't pay any attention when you tell me things. But that would be tactless. So I say, "I guess I forgot." Then I heave a long, bummed sigh. "Can't I just stay here? Pleeeeease? We'll just have a couple of people over, and I swear

Frankie and I will clean up everything. We were going to get all dressed up and be elegant, that's all. Pleeease?"

She pops her head out of another T-shirt. "Do I look like a moron?"

"No," I say, eyeing her shirt critically. "That one's good."

"No," she says. "That's not what I meant. What I meant was only a moron would leave two gorgeous fifteen-year-old girls alone in the house on New Year's Eve. I wasn't born yesterday, you know."

Major artillery is deployed: "Mom! Frankie and I are good kids! We never do *anything* sus. We're upstanding citizens. We're, like, the most boring people in the universe. All we want to do is dress up and have a dinner party, like old ladies—it's not like we're going to have a rager or anything. We would *never*. Have we ever gotten in trouble for *anything*? No. Come on, pleeeease. I'm too old to go to Granddad's." This is what my dad calls building the Mercedes to settle for the Chevy—ask for everything you want and allow yourself to be whittled back. Because that last part is true. Come on. Not that I don't love my granddad, but only eight-year-olds spend New Year's Eve with their grandparents.

Mom gives me this sarcastic look. "Not a chance, shorty."

Then there's a lot of moaning and complaining that's too long to repeat and I'm sure you can imagine anyway.

[Not to mention that writing conversations is a major

pain in the ass. Comma, quote, capital letter, period, quote, help! Whoever thought the rules up was a dick.]

When it finally ends, I've got the Chevy. Mom doesn't budge on me staying here with Frankie. But she does admit that I am kind of old to have to go to Granddad's, and she says she'll call Sharon to ask if I can spend the night over at Frankie's on New Year's Eve. I race to the phone to get Frankie on board, which she is. Maybe Max and Grant will go out to a club, she says. And we start planning what we'll eat, which is a little bit hard, because we don't really know how to make anything except for shortbread (me) and blondies (Frankie). But any deeker can make pasta, and besides, Sharon is always trying to teach Frankie to cook, so maybe she'll help us.

Cool! We're pumped.

For about twenty minutes.

Because after Mom talks to Sharon, and then Sharon talks to Tom, and then Sharon talks to Frankie, and then Sharon talks to Mom again, and then Mom talks to me, here's what Frankie and I have:

I can sleep over at Frankie's house on New Year's Eve instead of going to Granddad's, and we can have a "lovely" dinner party for two. No one else can come over because Sharon and Tom are going out to a party and won't be there to "supervise."

But—oh joy—Max says he'll keep an eye on us.

Yippee.

I'd call that a 1993 Chevy with two flat tires.

Why do I even bother being good?

Frankie and I have one of our many our-lives-suck phone conversations. "I still want to wear my dress," she says. "We can still have it be fancy, okay? And put on makeup and stuff." She sounds kind of desperate.

"Okay," I say slowly. "Why?"

"Because I'm tired of having no life!" she yells.

"Jeez. Calm down." I very kindly don't say Get real.

"No!!" she yells again

"Okay," I say, super-soothing. "We'll get all dressed up and eat fancy food. I'm into it."

"Good," she says, and hangs up.

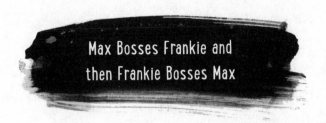

Max Bosses Frankie and then Frankie Bosses Max

Just as the rain began, Frankie came to a four-way intersection.

"Wipers," said Max.

She turned on the wipers. "I'm on the right, right?"

"Right."

Smoothly she accelerated through the intersection. "Very good," she said to herself.

"Make a left here," said Max.

"Left," she agreed, peering carefully in all directions for oncoming traffic. "Very good," she said under her breath as she completed the turn.

"How about some freeway driving?" suggested Max.

Frankie flicked on her signal, pulled the car slowly to the curb, and cut the motor.

"What're you doing?"

"I'm trying to prepare myself," she said. "You know, for the freeway." She took a deep breath.

"Exhale."

She exhaled. "I don't think I can deal with the freeway."

"Okay. We don't have to," Max said.

She gave him an annoyed look. "You're supposed to tell me I'll be fine. You're supposed to say I'm an amazing driver and I can absolutely handle the freeway."

"You're an amazing driver and you can absolutely handle the freeway," said Max.

"Now I don't believe you."

He sighed. "Girls are insane."

"Fuck you," she snapped.

"Oh, nice," he said. "Way to overreact."

"Sorry," she said grudgingly. "It's just that minute you disagree with a guy, they call you insane."

He squinted at her. "I was just kidding."

"Okay, but I hate that. It's sexist and controlling."

"Jesus." Suddenly Max leaned back in his seat, frowning. "Huh."

Frankie eyed him. "Did you call your girlfriend crazy?" she guessed.

He rubbed his face. "I can't remember the exact words. Maybe something like that."

"What about?" she asked cautiously. She didn't want to mess up. She'd never had this kind of a conversation with Max before.

"Ahh, I didn't want to go over to her house, and she got mad at me. She thinks I'm not spontaneous enough. Because I actually do my work. Unlike her. But anyway, she was trying to get me to come over and telling me that I was using music as an excuse not to see her and I said something like You're insane and then all of a sudden, she was raging. Whew. That was crazy."

"You just did it again. Asshole."

"Shit. Yeah. She almost broke up with me."

"Did you go over."

He nodded. "Eventually."

"Good move."

There was a pause. "She's still kind of mad at me."

He was almost asking her advice. Not quite, but almost. Carefully Frankie said, "About that? How long ago was it?"

"Not about that exact thing," Max said. He took a breath. "She thinks I'm not really into her. 'Uncommitted' is the word she used. Also 'uncaring.'"

"Really? But you do like her, right?"

"I really like her." He put his hands on the dashboard and cracked his knuckles.

"How come?"

He gave Frankie a suspicious look. "I just do. She's fun. She's not boring. She doesn't talk about stupid stuff."

"Is she cute?"

"See? That's exactly the kind of stupid shit she doesn't talk about!" he yelled.

"Oh my god, you're such a dick. I was just asking." Was it stupid? Frankie wondered. Maybe. Maybe he really didn't care what she looked like. "What does she talk about?"

"Lots of stuff. She has all these theories. She's the queen of theories. Most of them have no basis at all, but they're pretty funny."

"Like what?"

He smiled. "Like she thinks that people with really nice sheets and bedspreads are more depressed than people with just normal sheets."

Frankie giggled.

Max grinned at her. "I know. She's nuts. She says she's going to do a study and prove it. She's a psych major." He shook his head. "She has lots more. Theories." His smile faded. "She's going to break up with me."

"But Max," said Frankie, "if she's mad because you're uncaring, then she must like you."

He nodded. "I guess. Maybe. But she's sick of putting up with me."

"'Cause you don't hang out with her enough?"

He shrugged. "'Cause I can't just drop everything and be with her all the time."

"Are you really, uh, committed when you are with her?"

"Yeah, sure." He didn't sound sure.

"Have you told her how much you like her?"

"She knows."

"Have you told her?" Frankie pressed.

"Well. Not in so many words, maybe," he admitted.

"Oh. My. God. Are you kidding me?"

"Oh. My. God," he mimicked her.

"You're a moron." Frankie turned on the engine. "We are driving home right now and you're going to call her and tell her."

"Bossy cow."

"Loser."

But Frankie noticed that he didn't object to her plan. When they arrived at home, he went downstairs to his room and shut the door.

Displaying earth-shattering amounts of self-control, Frankie didn't ask a single question about how the conversation had gone when she saw her brother the next morning. She didn't even give him a meaningful raised-eyebrow So? But it didn't take a genius to see that he was in a good mood—he kept making little happy robot sounds, like *boop!* as he pottered around the kitchen getting his breakfast. And when he said, "So, freeway today, kid?" she knew that (a) his phone call had gone well and (b) he was giving her credit for it.

But all she said was, "Sounds good."

Her mom, who was trying find a recipe that Frankie could make for the New Year's Eve soiree, looked up from her cookbooks. "You are a nice brother, Max," she said. She turned to Frankie. "You are lucky to have such a nice brother, and I am lucky to have such a nice stepson who's willing to give up his time so I don't have a nervous breakdown."

"No problem," Max said with his mouth full.

"What about carbonara, honey?" asked Frankie's mom, returning to the cookbooks. "That's about as easy as it gets. You have to run around a lot at the last minute, but it's not hard."

"Yum," said Frankie. "Char'll love it. She loves unhealthy stuff."

"You have to have salad, too," said her mom sternly.

"Do they get any champagne?" asked Max.

"No, they do not, Max McCullough!" said Sharon. "And you had better promise you won't give them any or I'm going to stay right here at home and ruin everyone's fun."

"Okay, okay, just asking, just trying to understand the rules," said Max, holding his hands up. "No champagne. Got it!"

"That's right," snapped Frankie's mom, glaring at him. "They're fifteen." Still glaring, she looked down at the cookbook, and Frankie and Max exchanged quick glances. He winked.

I drove on the freeway!

> *U r still alive?*

Pretty much. Onramps freak me out

> *Probs gets easier each time*

Hoping. Chloe's having a kickback

> *When?*

Tonight

> *You going?*

Yag, you?

> *I'm invited?*

Hello? Why wd I tell you if you weren't?

> *She's your friend*

But you're my ride or die

> *Cool. What time?*

8:30?

> *KK. Meet here at 8:30*

Cu then

NOTHING

Here's what a kickback is supposed to be: ten or fifteen people sitting around listening to music, drinking, and eating chips. A few people hooking up. No big deal. Smooth.

Here's what Chloe's kickback is: eighty or ninety people jamming themselves into her house to get totally trashed and lose their minds, while about ninety more people lurk around in her yard, trying to get inside, even though they weren't invited. Trying to get inside includes breaking her kitchen window and attempting to break down the front door and then getting mad and drawing a big penis on her porch in Sharpie.

This is why I will never have a party at my house.

This is why I don't even want anyone to know where I live.

But god bless Chloe for not being me. She is putting on. I mean, parties are mostly like Bigfoot. Mythological. Everyone's always saying there's going to be one, and then you kill yourself to get there and it's twelve seniors glaring at you and telling you to get the fuck out. Or, it's lame. Or, it was last week. Or, in the one-in-ten event that it is a real party *and* you're invited *and* you can get there, you have a crappy time anyway. But Chloe's party is good. I am looking fabulous—I know I'm not supposed to say that, but I am—in my new scoop neck which I just got with one of my gift cards, plus Frankie and I engaged in some minor illicit activity while we were walking over, plus we feel really proud that we're allowed in while there are some juniors— wow, a lot of juniors—out there in the yard.

"Hey, Charlotte!" calls this kid I know named Mervin (poor guy). "Can you get me in? I'll smoke you out."

"Sorry, I'm a plus-one myself," I call back as the door opens and Chloe—looking kind of freaked, which is not surprising—lets us in.

But just as she's closing the door behind us, these two guys I don't know push in right behind us, the way you do when you're hopping a turnstile, and then drop down, so Chloe doesn't see them. She's talking to some other girl—hi,

Lisette—and so Frankie and I are the only ones who know they're there. We look down, just in time to hear one of them say to the other, "If I don't fuck something in thirty minutes, I'm outta here."

So I knee him as hard as I can in the shoulder and he falls over. And then Frankie starts laughing, and we sweep off, leaving him on the floor, where some drunk kid trips over him.

I feel good about myself.

The normal stuff happens—hi, Reed, hi, Johnny— and I go off to hang with a couple of friends of mine in the kitchen, where they are making this huge deal about smoking cigarettes (which is disgusting) and there's this completely silent kid sitting at the kitchen table, eating cereal, bowl after bowl. He's probably high. He's probably going to yak pretty soon. I don't want to be there when it happens, so I leave. I do some dancing and then I look around for Frankie.

And there she is, on the stairs, having a deep and meaningful conversation with one of the Chrises from her English class. Who she's told me numerous times is a complete dick. Huh. Now he's touching her hair. Huh again. He's going to kiss her. Yep, there he goes. Frankie appears to find this acceptable. You go, Franklin. I guess they're only complete dicks until they tell you you're hot. Or until you're desperate for something to happen.

I feel cynical. I turn cynically away and look around the

living room, which is a throbbing mass of bodies. There is a kid dancing on the dining room table. Poor Chloe. There are a bunch of people cacked out on the sofa. Poor Chloe's parents. Eden is one of the cacked out—hi, Eden—oh, wait, she's not completely cacked out. She's laughing at some guy who's leaning over her. Way over her.

It's the guy who wants to fuck something in thirty minutes.

He's talking to her, and she's laughing. Now he's trying to pull her up off the couch, but she's schmacked, so it ain't easy.

But it's not that hard, either. He's got his hand under her butt and he's sort of hoisting her and feeling her up at the same time.

Asshole.

I look quickly toward the stairs, to see if Frankie's seeing what I'm seeing. But fuck me, she's gone. Where the hell is she?

Eden's up, she's hanging on to the guy to keep from falling over.

He's kissing her neck and kind of moving her along toward the back door—what's he planning to do, fuck her in the yard in front of everyone?

Yes, I guess he is.

No way.

Goddammit, Frankie, why are you hooking up with a guy you don't like when I need you?

I don't have time to find her. Eden's got both arms around the guy now.

I start threading the needle—"'scuse me, sorry, hey, how are you, sorry, whoops, 'scuse me"—and I manage to get over to that side of the room before he gets Eden out the door. Then I go for it. "Eden! Oh my god! I've been looking for you all over!" I glance at the guy, who luckily doesn't recognize me, and say, "Hi! I'm a friend of Eden's and—sorry, I just have to borrow her for like one tiny minute because she has my"—I giggle—"tampons." Brilliant; he looks grossed out. "Can you just, like, come here a sec?" I say to Eden and put my hand on her arm. She looks really out of it, like she has no idea who I am.

"Hey, c'mon," says Asshole, kind of pissed. "She's with me."

"Yeah—" Eden looks vaguely at the guy. "With him."

"Okay, but I'm having kind of a blood issue," I say, and pull her toward me. She almost falls on me.

Asshole doesn't care that much—he's already looking down at the couch for another candidate—so I drag Eden away.

"Come on, Eden, let's get out of here," I say.

"I think I might barf," she says, extremely clearly. And then she does.

Poor Chloe.

* * *

I have been to Eden's house before, which is fortunate, because Eden apparently hasn't. "Where're we *going*?" she keeps moaning while we're walking there. "Where're we *going*?"

"We're going to your house."

"But it's *dark*," she moans.

I think she's talking about the fact that it's night, but when we get to her house, I decide that she's talking about her house. Because it is totally dark. Not a single light on.

"Do you have a key?" I ask.

"Flowerpot," she moans.

So I have to look under a bunch of flowerpots until I find the key. I let us in and switch on a few lights. "Where are your mom and dad?" I ask.

"LA."

"They left you by yourself?" I ask.

"Yeah."

"When are they coming back?"

She shakes her head. She doesn't know? "Next week," she says after a minute.

"Next *week*?" Some people have really crap parents. My parents won't even leave me alone for a night, which is annoying, but, you know, that's what parents are supposed to do.

Eden stretches out on the couch. I bring her some water.

(In the kitchen, I check the refrigerator. At least there's plenty of food in there). She drinks it. She falls asleep. I sit there and look at her.

Where'd you go?

   I'm at Eden's. I'll tell you tomorrow. You still at Chloe's?

   No. Police came

   I bet. When?

   Deek. Half hour ago?

   [I look at the time. 11:20. Another wild night in the big city.]

   How was Chris?

   Not as bad as I thought

   Ho

   FU

   Where are you?

   Home

   Lucky

   Wish you were here

   Yeah right

   What's the matter with you?

   Sorry. I'll tell you tomorrow.

I am now faced with a moral dilemma. It is currently 11:38. My curfew is midnight ('cause it's Christmas break). If I leave

Eden's at 11:45, I'll be home by midnight. Should I leave Eden? I look over at her, sleeping on the couch.

I don't think she's going to drown on her own vomit. She already got rid of almost everything on Chloe's rug. Poor Chloe.

But I also think that if I were a really good person, I'd call my mom and ask if Eden could spend the night at my house. Unfortunately, this would entail revealing that Eden is and/or was drunk. At the party I was attending. And this would lead to questions about consumption of alcohol and drugs at parties. And this in turn would lead to questions about my consumption of alcohol and drugs. Now. Ahem. I do not tell my parents the entire truth. The entire truth is: I'm pretty good. I'm not one hundred percent good, but I am pretty good. I smoke a little weed. I drink a beer or two sometimes, which I don't even like very much. But my parents wouldn't buy it. They'd think that if Eden did it, that means I do it, too. Then they'd start thinking that when I go to parties, I do the kind of things extreme kids do, yanking down lean and snorting coke, etcetera. And then they'd never let me out again. Parents have a hard time believing in moderation.

So I watch Eden breathe in and out for about ten minutes. Then I prop her up on some pillows, so that she won't choke on her own vomit in case I'm wrong. Then I put pillows down on the floor next to the couch, so if she falls off, she won't die.

And then I leave.

I should be feeling good because I saved Eden from being raped. But I don't feel good. I feel shitty.

Frankie Has Her Own Pre-Party

"So? Are you guys going to be a thing now?" asked Charlotte, busily stirring a mountain of sugar into her latte.

Frankie coughed foam. "What?"

"You and Chris," said Charlotte, still not looking at her.

"No!" Frankie said loudly. She put her cup down. "Why would you say that?"

Charlotte looked up. "I don't know. Maybe you're like, fiending for him and you forgot to tell me."

Frankie's eyes narrowed. "Are you pissed at me? For hooking up with Chris? Which, by the way, I wasn't."

"I'm not pissed," Charlotte said crisply. "You told me he

was a dick, but I guess you don't think that anymore."

Frankie turned a little red. "Excuse me? What the hell, Char? I mean, okay, I made out with Chris, but we were mostly just talking, and I don't see why you're tripping about it anyway."

"Talking, yeah, right," Charlotte said sarcastically.

"Fuck you, we were. We were actually talking about something that happened in English." Frankie folded her arms across her chest and glared at Charlotte. "I repeat, what's your problem?"

"I was just asking if you're going to be a thing now."

"And I said no. We're not. Were you a thing with Aidan after Gaby's party?"

Now Charlotte flushed. "That was a long time ago."

"August."

Charlotte didn't reply. She slid her latte back and forth over the tiny, dirty table. "I'm sorry," she said finally. "I guess I feel like there's stuff you're not telling me and it makes me feel bad."

Frankie frowned. "There's nothing I'm not telling you."

Charlotte rolled her eyes. "St. Albans?"

"Oh. Yeah. That. I knew you'd get upset, that's all."

"But that's what I mean," said Charlotte. "I got more upset when I found out, because you hadn't told me."

Frankie nodded. "I can't think of anything else I haven't

told you. Nothing's happened. Nothing's happening. It's not like I have a thrilling secret life, Char." She sighed. "I wish."

Charlotte looked down at the table. "I know you want me to be more exciting."

"Hello?" said Frankie. "I don't give a shit about whether you're exciting. I wish I was more exciting."

Charlotte laughed and relaxed against the back of her chair. "Good to know, dawg. So. No Chris?"

Frankie laughed, too. "Nah. He's better than I thought, though. I mean, he does have some good opinions about things. But I don't think he's into me anyway."

"He looked pretty into you."

"Well, maybe a little. But not long-term." Frankie snickered. "When he was, like, hugging me, he said, 'Dang, you're boney, girl.'"

"He did *not*!" Charlotte yelped.

"No, it was okay. It was funny. I mean, I laughed and so did he. But he's not that into me. It's okay. I'm not that into him, either."

For a few minutes, they drank their lattes and looked at their phones in companionable silence. "Eden's okay," said Charlotte, reading.

"Does she remember what happened?" asked Frankie.

"Not much. Think I should tell her?" asked Charlotte.

Frankie nibbled the edge of her cup, thinking. "I don't

know. You think she'd stop drinking that shit if she knew?"

Charlotte shrugged. "Got me. Who knows what Eden would do about anything?" She paused. "Maybe Chloe will tell her. Because of the rug."

"Yeah."

More texting.

"Franklin?"

Frankie looked up. "Yag?"

Charlotte was busily stirring her latte again. "Just so you know, Sid sent me a drawing for Christmas. It's a porcupine and it's really cute. That's all. It's no big deal."

Frankie raised her eyebrows. "When did this happen?"

"Couple days ago."

"Why you didn't tell me?"

Charlotte sighed. "I didn't want you to tell me to fight the fight, okay? I wanted you to know, but I didn't want you to make a big deal about it."

"Okay." Frankie looked hurt.

Charlotte sighed again. "It's just—there's nothing I can do about Sid, Frankie. Okay?"

Frankie nodded. "Okay." She waited. "I feel like you don't trust me."

Charlotte drew her finger across the dirty table. "I feel like you wish I was different."

Frankie opened her mouth and then closed it. "Not for

me," she said finally. "For you, I wish you were different, but for me, you're perfect."

Charlotte smiled. "Okay. But then again, you're psycho."

"Even at Starbucks, you're not supposed to take a table for *hours*," huffed a nearby voice.

Charlotte and Frankie looked up from their phones, startled, to find a lady in a rumpled business suit glaring at them. Charlotte glanced at the table beside them, where a middle-aged man wearing a headset was having a conversation while typing on his computer. He'd been there when they'd arrived.

The lady raised her eyebrows and sighed loudly.

They looked at each other and shrugged. "I kind of have to eat anyway," said Charlotte. "My mom says if we want chocolate cake for tonight, we have to make the cake part this morning so it'll be cool enough to frost by the middle of the afternoon."

"Okay. What time are you coming over?" asked Frankie, rising.

"People are *supposed* to bus their own cups!" snapped the lady.

"Jesus," said Charlotte under her breath. She picked up her cup. "I think five or five thirty."

"Okay," said Frankie. "You want me to put your hair up? I'm going to put my hair up."

"People are *waiting!*" said the lady so loudly that the man with the headset jumped.

Frankie and Charlotte rolled their eyes at each other and moved away from the table.

"About time," puffed the lady. "Act like they own the place."

"Have a great day!" called Charlotte over her shoulder. "Happy New Year!"

"Pff!" said the lady, slapping a stack of folders down on the dirty table.

Frankie's house was on a hill. The downside: a pretty steep walk to get there, followed by forty-four stairs up to the front door. The upside: the view. From her living room window, you could see out over the entire bay, across to the city and to the Zayante Ridge, rising above the water on the other side of the bridge. Frankie decided that she and Charlotte would have their fancy dinner in the living room, so they could see all of it. Her mother helped her put up a little table, and Frankie went to town setting it with a white tablecloth and napkins, candles, and her mom's first-marriage silverware.

"Good thing I didn't go for the monogram," Sharon said unsentimentally, looking at Frankie's work. "It looks elegant, sweetie, but now let's go to the kitchen so I can make sure you know what you're supposed to do."

Pasta, check. Water, check, Eggs, check. Cheese, check; cream, check; bacon, check. Salad, check. Dressing, check. Check, check, check. Frankie stopped listening until she heard her mother say, "Okay, I think that's it, then. I'm going to go get dressed."

"This early? It's only four thirty."

Her mom looked at her in irritation. "I just said your daddy wants to leave at five. I just said it. Were you listening to me?"

"Oh! Right!" said Frankie hastily. "I think I'll go get dressed, too!"

She was still in process a half an hour later when her mom knocked on her door.

"Yeah!" called Frankie

Her mom poked her head in. "Wow!" she said. "You look—old."

Frankie grinned. "Don't I?"

Her mother shook her head. "If you're old, I'm older."

"You look incredible, Mom," said Frankie.

"So do you. Give me a kiss, sweetie. We're leaving."

"Are you going to be out late?" asked Frankie hopefully.

Her mom raised an eyebrow. "You know your father. He doesn't like to stay up. I'll be surprised if we make midnight."

"Whoa, savage."

"Now, I want you to know that I've made it entirely clear to Max that he is not to leave you and Charlotte on your own for any reason and that I expect all of you to follow the rules."

"Yes, Mommy," said Frankie mechanically. "Honest to god, nothing's going to happen to us. Nothing ever happens to us."

"And that's the way we want it," said her mother. She kissed Frankie. "Be a good girl."

"Yes, Mommy," said Frankie again. "Have fun."

The house was quiet when Frankie emerged from her room. Max and Grant were downstairs somewhere—probably sleeping or listening to music, which was what they mostly did. Frankie drifted through the kitchen, the dining room, her father's office, the hallway, and then to the bathroom to look at herself in the mirror again. In the dimming light, her skin was pale, her eyes were huge, and her hair was a dark, graceful swirl. It was like catching a glimpse of herself in the future. She turned from one side to the other, wishing someone was there to see her. Who? Charlotte? Nah. Charlotte always told her she was beautiful, even when she was wearing sweats. She tried to work up a daydream about Chris appearing suddenly at the door, but it didn't jell. Still, she thought, turning this way and that, I look gorgeous.

She left the mirror and went across the hall into the living room, to the window facing the bay, where the sky was ablaze with pink and gold and purple. Talk about gorgeous, she thought, watching the light change. She went out the front door to the wide open deck, where the sky seemed to be pulsing as if it had a heartbeat. Happy New Year to me, she thought dreamily as footsteps sounded on the stairs. Charlotte. "Come up here," Frankie called softly. "You've got to see this."

The footsteps stopped, but when Frankie turned, it wasn't Charlotte. It was a man she'd never seen before. He was young, but a man, not a kid, and he was standing motionless at the edge of the deck, staring at her with his dark eyes wide.

Frankie said nothing. Not for any of the usual reasons she didn't talk—shy, scared, embarrassed—but because it felt almost magical to have him look her with such wonder in the glowing light. She gazed calmly back at him.

Without saying a word, he took a step toward her and held out his hand. Somehow, it seemed perfectly normal for Frankie to do the same, and their hands met.

"Hi," he whispered. And then he put two fingers very lightly along her jawbone and bent to give her a lingering kiss. When, at last, he pulled away, he still held her cheek in his warm hand.

There was a thump. "What the hell are you doing, Dobranski?" yelled Max, on the other side of the window. He thumped the glass again.

Frankie and the man looked at one another and smiled. "Am I in trouble?" he murmured.

Max stormed out the front door with a beer in one hand.

"Jesus Christ, Zack, that's my sister! She's fifteen!"

Zack's eyes moved over her face, and he shook his head in amazement. "My bad," he said to Frankie gently, releasing her hand. He glanced at Max. "You've got to admit, she doesn't look fifteen."

"Take my word for it, she's fifteen. Aren't you?" Max glared at Frankie.

She nodded. She couldn't stop smiling.

"Stop smiling." Max folded his arms across his chest over his beer bottle. "What the fuck, man?"

"Sorry. I was"—Zack turned to smile again at Frankie—"I don't know what came over me."

"Look, if you're going to hit on my fifteen-year-old sister, I'm going to kick you out."

Zack put his hands up. "I'm not going to hit on her. I'm going to look at her one more time"—he turned his head and did that—"and then I'm not going to look at her anymore. Or touch her, either." He exhaled slowly. "I might think about her, though."

"Cut it out," said Max. "No thinking. You've got to leave her alone, Zack. Really, I'm serious."

"Yeah, okay," said Zack. "I will. I swear." He looked at Frankie one more time and closed his eyes. "I'm here to play music."

Max turned to Frankie. "Do I need to kick him out? I don't

want to, but I will if you can't handle it."

Could Frankie handle it? Of course she could! She had never felt more powerful in her life. She could handle anything. "You don't need to kick him out. Char's going to be here in a minute, and you won't even see us unless you come upstairs."

"We're not going to," said Max firmly. "Come on."

"Bye," said Zack. He gave her a little smile. "See you in about five years."

"I'm going to kick your ass, Dobranski. Come on. Downstairs."

Frankie heard the conversation switch to guitars as they went downstairs. She turned to face the bay once more and found that the sun had somehow set without her. Wow! She took a deep breath, and then she began to chuckle.

"What?" It was Charlotte, holding an enormous cake on a platter. She was wearing a very small black skirt and a very tight white sweater that Frankie had never seen before. Around her neck was a black silk ribbon.

"Whoa," Frankie said. "Beyond."

"That means good, right?" said Charlotte's mother, thumping up the stairs behind her with a duffel bag.

Charlotte rolled her eyes. "Right."

"And dank means bad?" her mother went on, frowning in concentration.

"Dank means *good*," Charlotte said.

"But bad means good too," Frankie volunteered. Charlotte glanced at her in surprise.

Charlotte's mother shook her head and dropped the duffel bag by the front door. "No wonder you're all insane," she said. "Is your mom home, Frankie?"

"Nope, they already left," Frankie said. "Max is here, though, if you want to talk to him."

"No, that's okay. I'll talk to the two of you. Now"—she turned to face them—"there will be no leaving this house until tomorrow morning, right?"

"Right," said Charlotte.

"There will be—"

"Nobody allowed in the house while Sharon and Tom are gone," recited Charlotte. "There will be no drinking. No drugs. No teenage pregnancy."

"Right!" said her mother. She turned to Frankie. "Right?"

"We'll do our best," giggled Frankie, and again, Charlotte raised a surprised eyebrow.

Charlotte's mother, on the other hand, seemed unfazed. "There will be good behavior. Am I right?"

"Yes, Mommy," said Charlotte, just as Frankie had.

There were kisses and good-byes and Happy New Years, and after that, Charlotte's mother thumped away, down the stairs.

"I love your ribbon thing," said Frankie happily as they walked into the house.

"Did you smoke without me?" asked Charlotte, looking at her closely.

"No!" said Frankie. "I am clean and sober."

Charlotte narrowed her eyes. "What's with you, then? You look fantastic, by the way. But you seem bizarrely—I don't know—cheerful."

Frankie grinned. "You won't even believe what just happened."

NOTHING

"You won't even believe what just happened," says Frankie.

And she is right. I don't believe it. Is it believable that a guy she's never seen before in her life suddenly appears—ta-da!—on her front porch at the exact same moment that she happens to be out there in her best dress all alone and then—*without talking*—they walk toward each other and he just bends down and kisses her? And she *lets* him? And it's totally sexy and not gross and weird and awkward?

No, it is not believable.

And then Max sees, and he yells at the guy, and still, neither of them is embarrassed or freaked out?

And then the guy just goes downstairs?

And he's still down there?

Not believable.

Frankie laughs. "You'd believe it if it was in one of your teen books."

"If it was in a teen book, the two of you would be having sex in your room right now, and I'd be sitting all by myself in the living room, having an eating disorder."

"No." Frankie giggles. "You'd be cutting yourself with my mom's fancy silverware."

And it is this, more than anything, that makes me believe her. The laughing. She's, uh, I guess *radiant* is the word. On top of the world, as my dad would say. Exhilarated. I am suspicious, as usual. I am also probably a little jealous. A lot jealous. "So. Are you going to be leaving me alone in the living room later on, so you can go downstairs and hook up with him?"

She shakes her head. "No. I told Max I wouldn't. Besides, it'd be creepy if he hooked up with me knowing that I'm a kid. Then I wouldn't like him. Nah. It was just a great moment."

I stare at her, wondering what it must be like, how she must feel. "Not a plot twist that's going to change the rest of your life?"

She laughs again and shakes her head. "Just—fun."

"You seem really happy," I say.

She whacks the kitchen counter with a wooden spoon for

a moment, and then she says, "It makes me feel like things I don't expect can actually happen. And like life is going to get more interesting than it is right now. Like there might actually be some potential." She looks at me. "So, yeah, I'm happy."

"I would be, too," I say, and I am totally sincere about this, even though I think a man appearing on your porch and kissing you is kind of an outlier, statistically, and I don't think I'd base my worldview on it. "How old is he, do you think?"

"Deek. Twenty? He's a friend of Max's, so college age. But he seemed a little older than Max."

"Yeah," I say. "Can't really picture Max walking up to someone and kissing her in manly silence."

She giggles. "Me neither. Besides, Max has a girlfriend."

I nod and look around the kitchen at all the yummy-looking stuff that—I'm pretty sure—Sharon has laid out for us. "I'm getting hungry."

Frankie whacks the counter again. "Let's do it!" She is peppy as hell.

Frankie and I are lame-os. We run around and crash into each other and spill the cream and have to cook the pasta twice (not the same pasta) because we have a little cognitive problem with the colander. We forget the salad and then remember it after the pasta's done (the second time), and then we (I) toss it too hard and it goes over the side of the counter, and we

(Frankie) get scared of the frying pan and pour a lot of fancy Italian grease all over the pasta, which we (I) don't think is really supposed to be there. But, finally, we sit down in the living room at the pretty table, in the candlelight, and maybe it isn't the best spaghetti I've ever eaten, but it's really good, and we are proud. We eat a ton, but we are elegant, too, and we're looking at the lights come on in the city and we're talking about things we used to do for New Year's when we were little, like how I couldn't believe that I was actually allowed to bang pots together; it seemed like something I'd get in deep shit for, but no, the grown-ups stood around, gazing fondly at me while I made total fucking mayhem. Frankie had this really sad memory of her creepy brother Leland telling her it was New Year's when it wasn't. They made all this confetti together and threw it at her parents, and her mom cried.

Anyway, we are having conversations and it's an elegant dinner, and we agree that we are having a way better time than we would be if we were doing what everyone else is doing, which is going to Reed's dad's apartment to play video games (except for Noony, who's in Texas). We take a lot of pictures of how great we look by candlelight and put some up, and we get like, sixty-three likes in about eight minutes, including from Johnny, Merle, Chris, Cora, Kellen, Chloe, and Sid, which not only means that we are hot, but also that they are not at the most amazing party in the world that everyone's invited to except us. So we've got us a FOMO-free New Year's here. Cool.

We are still proud and happy even when it's time to clean up. We play our current songs and dance around and clean the burners, because we are wonderful human beings. Plus, we still have chocolate cake (thank you, Charlotte) and movies to go! All our old favorites are in the lineup: *Mean Girls*, *500 Days of Summer*, *Easy A*, and this movie Frankie loves called *Caterpillar Spring*, about a guy who runs away from home on his backhoe (pause while we lose our shit about the word *backhoe*).

It's 11:00—no, it's 11:08—and Frankie and I are snuggled on the couch in our sweatpants, watching *Caterpillar Spring*, when we hear someone coming upstairs.

Frankie mutes. "Who's that?" she calls, a little nervously. Because what if this guy *is* a creep who would try to get something going on even though he knows she's fifteen? (I'll protect you, I think. I am Charlotte, defender of local virginity.)

Max sticks his head in the door. "Me."

She relaxes. "Are you guys hungry? There's leftover pasta in the kitchen." She hesitates. "There might not be enough for three people."

Max makes a face. "It's just me."

"Where'd Grant and, uh, Zack go?"

"To the city." He looks bummed.

"They went without you?" asks Frankie. "That's kind of fucked-up."

"I can't go," Max says. "I have to stay with you guys."

"Ohhh. Right," says Frankie.

"Sorry," I add.

"Do you want some leftover pasta?" offers Frankie apologetically.

He sighs. "I already had pizza." He looks at the plates on our laps. "Is that cake?"

"Yeah. It's really good," says Frankie.

"Help yourself," I say. "There's tons more."

"And then come watch movies with us, if you want," Frankie says, trying to make it up to him for ruining his New Year.

"Maybe," he says. He goes off, and I think we won't see him again, but he comes back in a few minutes with the biggest piece of cake in the world and some milk. He sits down in a chair and starts wolfing cake, and Frankie turns the movie up and we watch together.

It's a pretty good movie—this kid is in love with this girl, and the only way he can get to her is to drive his backhoe, like, a hundred miles. At night he sleeps under it, and people keep trying to steal it—but none of them are really mean about it and they help him and stuff. Finally he gets there, and the girl turns out to be at camp, so he doesn't get her after all, and he has sex with her mom instead. Then he drives home. The end.

"Okay, that is a weird ending," I say. "Why does he do her mom, if he's so in love with the girl."

"He doesn't even know the girl, hardly," says Frankie. "It's all a—not a dream, but the other thing—a *projection*. So he might as well do the mom."

"Why would the mom do him?" I ask. "He's just this little dweeb."

"Maybe she thinks he's cute," says Frankie.

"Maybe she's trying to regain her lost youth," I say. "Or maybe the whole thing is a male fantasy."

"Harsh," says Max. But he's smiling.

"Just wait till she gets going," says Frankie. "She's totally cynical."

"I'm not," I say. "I love everyone."

"You are *such* a fucking liar."

We laugh.

"Hang on," says Max. He gets up and we hear him go downstairs. He comes back in a minute with an open bottle of champagne. Frankie and I exchange looks of excitement.

"Really?" she asks him. "We can have some?"

He peers into the bottle. "Grant already drank about half of it. But yeah. It's New Year's, right?"

I glance at the clock on the TV. It is 11:57. "Run get glasses!" I tell Frankie. "Quick!"

She runs away and returns with three glasses. Max carefully pours them out so they're all evenly full, and then, at exactly twelve o'clock midnight we lift our glass and say, "Cheers!" and take a sip of champagne. Which I like.

"It's better when it's colder," says Max.

"Chill, man," says Frankie. Which for some reason they both find hilarious. Maybe they're lightweights.

We are just finishing our champagne when there is a rumbling noise below the house—is this an earthquake that will change Nothing into a dramatic tale of survival? No. It's Frankie's garage. Her parents are home. 12:14 p.m. Way to par-tay, Tom and Sharon. Max laughs and takes his champagne bottle downstairs, while Frankie races the glasses into the kitchen to wash and dry and put them back on the shelves. Max reappears and says, "You guys can come down and finish it up later if you want."

But now Sharon and Tom are cracking the hall door, so there is a flurry of parental questions about the quality of our evening and exclamations about what great cleaners we are and groans of exhaustion because it's now 12:22 and apparently that is just the end for Tom and Sharon. They go staggering off to their room and close the door, and then Sharon staggers back to say they're going to sleep in tomorrow, which is, I guess, a major revolution, because they usually get up at 5:30, even on weekends. Weirdos.

● ● ●

Once they are tucked away, we go creeping down to Max's lair, which is, wow, really lairlike, with guitars and a keyboard and, weirdly, an oboe, not to mention a couch and a big chair and a TV and a desk and—dang, what *is* that?—a king-sized bed over in a kind of separate part of the room.

"You got stiffed," I say to Frankie. "Your room isn't nearly this good." Jeez—he's even got the view. I guess we're under the living room.

Frankie and Max both laugh. "They did it for Lee," she says. "They were thinking that he wouldn't be so—" She looks at Max for the right word.

"Difficult," he says.

She snickers. "Difficult, if he had his own space."

"Didn't really work," adds Max.

There's a pause. "You and Lee are so different," she says.

He nods. "Yeah. Lee's a trip."

"Think it was—?" She jerks her head upward, toward her mom and dad.

He shakes his head kind of sadly. "I don't know. Probably. But he was always pretty uptight. One of the first things I remember is him trying to smother me, and that was way before Dad bailed."

Frankie winces.

"And part of it's got to be genetics," says Max. "Lee's like Mom and Dad on steroids."

"Yeah. Poor Lee."

"Nice room, though," I volunteer.

Max nods—he's gotten much better-looking, I notice—and says, "Want to kill the champagne?"

"Yes!" Frankie and I say together, and he laughs.

"Sharon would freak if she knew I was doing this," he says, looking around the room for cups.

"Yeah, yeah," says Frankie. "She did stuff when she was young, too. She went out with a twenty-two-year-old when she was sixteen. You want me to go get cups?"

"Yeah," he says. They're funny people, Frankie and Max. I know they just had a real conversation, but they sure don't use very many words. In my house, everyone talks all the time, blah, blah, blah. Nobody shuts up. I think we probably are not saying anything very meaningful, or anything more meaningful than Frankie and Max just did, but there is a lot more noise. Frankie comes back with juice glasses (more innocent-looking) and—yay!—her stash.

"Dro!" I say happily.

"Happy New Year!" she says. "Max? You want some?"

"Sure," he says. We sip our juice glasses of champagne and Frankie rolls, which she is very talented at. "I can't believe my little sister is smoking me out," he says.

"Don't feel like you have to," she says. "No pressure here."

He laughs. "You get it from the skater kids still? Those guys over in the park?"

She nods, concentrating on her joint.

"Was Lefty around when you were there?" I ask. Lefty is this big dude with no left hand. He is an amazing skater and everyone loves him. He is also a major drug source.

Max laughs again. "Shit, he's still there? He's got to be at least twenty."

"He only goes to class about four times a year," I say. "It takes a while to graduate when you do it that way."

We down our tiny glasses of champagne and light up, and then Max says he's going to watch a movie and we can stay and watch it with him if we want, and we *do* want, even though it's *Iron Man 3* and we've seen it, like, twelve times, and it was pretty dumb the first time. We are laughing, and then Max gets the munchies and goes upstairs for his second incredibly enormous piece of cake and then we watch the movie and then Frankie falls asleep, which is reasonable because it's now about one thirty, and then I look over and Max is asleep, too, and then I'm yawning, and I bet you know what happens next.

Frankie Saves the Day.
She Really Does.

Frankie heard someone say, "Look, I'm *sorry*." Was it a dream? She shifted her head slightly and felt an unfamiliar bump under her neck. Shoot. Not a dream. "What else do you want me to say?" she heard. "You want me to say I'm dick? Okay, I'm a dick. I fucked up." It was Max.

Frankie opened her downward eye. She was on Max's couch. Her head was—ouch—resting on the arm of the couch. She opened her upward eye. The sky was a heavy gray. It was morning. It was probably not very late morning, though. She tried to focus at least one of her eyes on the tiny TV clock. Impossible. She burrowed a hand into her bra and took out her phone: 8:06.

"Oh, come on." Max sounded pissed. "I'm not allowed to make a mistake? Look—yeah, I know—okay, but that's you." Pause. "I'm not saying that, you're saying that."

Slowly Frankie unbent her knees and felt a big, warm lump against her shin. Charlotte. Frankie lifted her head to look. Fast asleep.

"No. You know what I was doing. I was babysitting my sister and her friend. Fine. Nothing I can do about that. Think what you want. Fine." Pause. "Really?" Pause. "That's what you want?" His voice thickened. "Okay." Pause. "Bye."

Silence.

Cautiously Frankie lifted her head to look toward her brother's bed. He was sitting on the edge of the mattress, staring at the floor. She saw his shoulders rise up as he took a deep breath. Very quietly, Frankie swung her legs off the couch and stood. He didn't notice her until she sat down on the floor in front of him.

"Was that Raina?" she said softly.

He nodded, still looking at the floor.

Frankie waited. Nothing. "What happened?" she asked finally.

"I don't want to talk about it," he said. His voice was rough.

"Yeah you do," she said instantly.

He glared at her. His eyes were red. "She just broke up with me, okay? So I'm not feeling really great right now."

"Why?"

"Why what?"

"Why'd she break up with you?"

Pause. "Because I forgot to call her last night."

Frankie tried not to give him a you-moron look. "You forgot?"

He sighed. "Yeah. I know. I'm an asshole. I get it. I just, like, wasn't thinking about it." He gave her a dark look. "I was babysitting."

"FU," said Frankie evenly. "And she was mad?"

"Yeah."

"I bet she was more hurt than mad. Disappointed and all that."

"No," he said bitterly. "Mad is what she was."

"You sounded pretty mad, too," Frankie pointed out.

"Nice you're on my side," he said.

Pause.

"I know you said you were sorry," Frankie said, "but I was over there on the couch and you didn't sound very sorry. You sounded, um, pretty defensive."

"I felt like she was attacking me," he protested. "I mean, I apologized. What else am I supposed to do?"

Frankie rolled her eyes at him. "Tell her you're sorry like

you're sorry. Tell her she's the greatest and you miss her. Jesus."

"I did all that," Max said sullenly.

"No, you didn't," Frankie said. She hesitated. "I don't get it. You're fine at apologizing around here. You're really nice and easy. Why are you such a hardass when you talk to her?"

He shook his head.

She kicked him gently on the ankle. "It's because you really like her, isn't it?" She nodded, agreeing with herself. "You're scared because she has so much power over you."

"Shut up," he said. But he gave her little smile. "I get enough psychology from her." Pause. "Or I did, anyway."

"Max." He looked at her. "I hate to say this, but you're a tap."

"Thanks."

"No, really. You really like her, and you act like a dick to her, *because* you really like her. That is just fucked-up. That is typical guy bullshit."

Max put his hands over his eyes and groaned. "I *know*." He shook his head. "I can't believe I fucked it up like this."

Frankie felt herself getting angry. "So? Grow a pair and call her back. Tell her you love her—you know you do—and stop being a dick."

Max looked at the phone in his hands. "What if she doesn't answer?"

"Then—where is she?"

"Some little town up north."

"In California?"

He nodded.

"So if she doesn't pick up, go get her! Jesus Christ! She's, like, a few hours away!" Frankie felt like hitting him.

"Good thing you're not a hardass," Max muttered, but he was going to his Recents at the same time. Frankie watched his face as he waited. One. Two. Th— "Raina?" he said. Frankie let out a relieved breath. "Hi. I don't want to break up." He stood and went into his bathroom and shut the door.

Frankie moved back to the couch and lay down, watching the leaden sky. There was no going back to sleep; she was wide awake. Happy New Year to me, she thought.

She heard a click and swiveled around to look at him. He was smiling. She lifted her eyebrows in a question. He nodded happily. "Good job," she called softly, and stood.

"You guys need to get out of here," he said. "I've got to get dressed."

"Go fuck yourself, I saved your relationship," said Frankie. "Get dressed in the bathroom."

He grinned. "Okay."

"How come you have to get dressed right this second anyway?"

"I'm going up there to get her," he said, his eyes shining.

"Thank you, Frankie," she said.

"Thank you, Frankie," he repeated obediently. He picked up a jacket. "She was like, crying when I called. She didn't want to break up, either. And she said it was partly that she's having such a shitty vacation. I mean, that's why she was so upset."

"Why's she having a shitty vacation?"

"Her stepmom doesn't like her, and her dad doesn't stand up for her."

"Oh. That's too bad." Frankie hesitated, an idea forming in her mind. "Max?"

"Huh?"

"She's coming back here with you? Like, to stay?"

"Yeah."

"What about Grant?"

"Grant?" said Max carelessly. "He can stay with Zack. Or Nabai. Besides, he's got to go see his dad for a couple of days. 'Cause Dad pays the bills."

"And where's this town Raina lives in?"

"It's—here, I can show you." Max sat down on the bed and pulled his laptop toward him. "It's up here, off the 5. McCloud, it's called. Lemme see"—he clicked keys, making his happy-robot noises—"not bad. It's only about four hours away."

"Can I see?" Frankie held her hand out for the laptop and

did a little clicking of her own while Max disappeared into the bathroom.

When he came out, she closed the laptop. "Hey."

"Hey." He bustled about, putting on socks. "She says it's cold up there."

"Yeah. Max, can Char and I go with you?"

He frowned. "No. Get out of here. Why?"

"Come on, it's not like you have to get a room the minute you see her!" Max blushed and Frankie continued, "You're bringing her back here anyway. So we'd just be coming along for the ride. We'd keep you company. I could even help you drive! Also, girls like guys who are nice to their sisters. We'll make you look good!"

"Well. Okay," he said slowly. "I guess you can. If you want to. Why would you want to?"

"New Year's Day is the most boring day of the year. It's a perfect day for a road trip. Plus, we like you! We want to spend time with you!"

Max glanced over at Charlotte's sleeping form. "I can see that. Okay, you can go, but you have to be ready in half an hour."

NOTHING

I am in a very nice place involving a lake and a lot of cute ducks when I am rudely interrupted.

"Wake up, you bum."

It's Frankie. She is shaking me, not very gently.

"Getup, getup, getup," she chants.

"No," I groan. I have to find this one duck. I roll over and slap around for a pillow to put over my head, but I don't have a pillow. Why don't I have a pillow? I lurch up and yell something along the lines of "What? What?"

Frankie starts laughing at me. "Dude looks like a la-dy!" she bellows.

Stupid Aerosmith. "Meanie," I mumble, and drop back down. "Why do I have to get up?"

"Because we're going on a road trip to reunite Max and his girlfriend. They already had a fight and broke up and got back together this morning, and he's going to go up and rescue her from her wicked stepmother."

"Wow." I look at the ceiling. "What time is it?"

"Nine."

"That's a lot of action for only nine," I say. "When are we going?"

"Now!"

Now turns out to mean in an hour. Because I have to wash my face and get dressed and brush my teeth and then get dressed again because Max's girlfriend lives up where it's cold. Plus, Sharon says she has a responsibility to make sure I eat breakfast even if her own children are idiots, so I have to sit down and eat (Max and Frankie heave dramatic sighs, but they also choke down a lot of toast, too). Unlike me, Frankie can function without coffee, but she is such a good friend that she tells her mom she really needs some, so Sharon makes a pot and we all gulp it down. While we are gulping, I text friendly New Year greetings to Mom and Dad, asking them interested questions about their night at the beach and slipping in an announcement about the road trip concept too. But there is no problem. *If it's okay with Sharon, it's okay with us, we trust Max, have fun,*

Mom texts, *drive safe, beach beautiful But cloudy, we'll be back tomorrow afternoon around 2, Granddad says he and Ollie had fun love and kisses, Robin says hi.*

All this with one finger.

We pile into the car. We pile out of the car and get some extra jackets and a blanket, which Frankie says we need for some reason. We pile back into the car. Max forgot his wallet. Oops! I should take my purse. And my charger. So should Frankie. We pile out of the car. Sharon has packed us some lunch. We pile back into the car. Wait! We should bring some leftover cake! We are about to pile out again, when Sharon comes running down the steps with a container. She thought we should take some cake. We love Sharon! Max starts the car. Tom comes running down the stairs. Max rolls down the window.

"Go get the girl, son!" Tom says, and gives Max a thumbs-up.

"Dad!" Frankie yells.

And we're off.

You want to know what's ugly? Freeways. Maybe there are pretty freeways somewhere, but not in California. They're covered with garbage and pathetic stuff that people have thrown out of their cars, like blankets and sofas. The sofas bum me out. I mean, think about it—at one point, someone picked out that sofa, thinking, This here is a good-looking sofa. How 'bout those purple flowers! And then it was in their house for fifteen years and then they gave it to their cousin who died and her rotten children stuck it in their house and finally when it was a sagging, ripped-up mess, they drove it to the freeway in the middle of the night and dumped it. And there it is, with its poor old purple flowers, upside down in the dirt. That is so fucking depressing.

I share these reflections with Sid. He says he agrees. Then he says we should start a Save the Sofa movement. We could go around picking up sofas off the side of the road and then we'd put them in a giant field like they do old horses, so they could live out their days in peace. Old people could go and sit in them, too.

He's so great.

I tell him I feel better now.

Good

I lean over the front seat to let Frankie in on the conversation. She reads it and nods. "Good idea," she says.

"Isn't he the greatest?" I sigh.

"The greatest," she agrees, because she is my main. She looks over at Max, driving. "But you're okay, too."

"Thanks," he says. "Who's the greatest?"

"This guy Charlotte is having a textual relationship with. Sid," says Frankie, and I stare at her because that's weird, letting Max know my personal stuff. Not necessarily bad, but weird. And then she goes on. "But she's never met him. She's never even seen him, because he doesn't put his picture up on the internet."

"Jeez, good for him," says Max.

"Why do you say that?" I ask, interested.

"Because it's shallow and everyone posts these fake pictures of themselves looking perfect. It's a waste of time."

"Wow," says Frankie. "You rebel."

"Probably it's because he has two noses," I say, kind of brooding.

Max laughs. "Yeah, that's probably it."

"Really, it's probably acne," I say.

"Could be," he says. This is not exactly comforting. "But then again, maybe he really doesn't believe in it." More comforting.

"Charlotte thinks she's never going to meet him even though they text like twenty-five times a day," Frankie goes on. "Right, Char?"

I look at her suspiciously. "Why are you telling Max all this, Frankie? Is this part of the Fight the Fight campaign? I told you, I don't want to hear that."

Frankie ignores me. "Char says that since she can't drive and he can't drive and her parents won't let her get on a train or a plane alone and he hasn't suggested doing those things, either, they're never going to meet."

"Frankie!" I yell. "What's your problem? Leave me alone!"

"I am," she says. "I'm just telling Max what you think. I'm updating him on your ideas. Charlotte thinks it's ridiculous to even be interested in the guy because she has no way to meet him."

Max glances over at her, kind of frowning. "I think you're upsetting Charlotte, Frankie." He means Shut up. Thank you, Max.

"Okay," she says. "I'll shut up." She's pretty damn cheerful about it, too. She starts looking through her phone. "Do we want Drake or Aerosmith?"

"Neither," says Max.

Then they argue about music while I do some more brooding.

I take it back. This part of the freeway is pretty. They've got the mountain thing going big-time up here, with genuine snow-covered peaks. Nice. Foresty. [Not exactly the most beautiful description, but you know what? I hate descriptions. "The stony mountain peaks were cloaked in a mantle of purple light." Yeah, yeah, tell someone who cares.]

"Are we almost there?" I yell because I'm too lazy to lean over the front seat.

"I think so," Frankie says. She looks at Max. "He's getting all excited."

"Shut up," he says.

Now we are on a different road. It's a "Scenic Byway," by golly. Who decides these things? Is it a job?

"Here," says Max, tossing his phone to Frankie. "Tell me how to get there."

I guess we must be almost there.

"I think you're supposed to go right here," says Frankie, squinting at the screen. "Were supposed to go right there," she adds as we pass the road.

"You've got to give me a little more notice than that," says Max, pulling over. "Hand me the phone." Now he's squinting. "You're full of shit. We don't turn until here. See? We're here." Frankie leans over to peer at the screen. Huh. You can sort of tell that they're brother and sister. I've never thought that before. They figure it out and Max pulls back on the road. So this is a road trip. I like it. It's boring, but in a good way.

He turns. Then he and Frankie gripe at each other and he turns again. Left and up. Wow. We're high. There aren't that many houses. I'd hate to live out here. There is not one goddamn thing to do. Unless you're into fishing or some such shit. Now Max is slowing down. Now he's craning his head, trying to see house numbers on mailboxes. Now he's pulling off the road beside a long driveway. He kills the engine.

Silence. Then he turns to Frankie. "Okay?"

"Beyond."

Oh my gosh, he was asking how he looked! That is so adorable! He takes a deep breath and gets out of the car. "Just stay here, okay?"

Frankie and I nod enthusiastically. We support young love. Go, Max!

He disappears down the driveway.

"How long do you think it's going to take?" I ask.

Frankie turns around. "Deek. Watch out, I'm coming back." She does the worm over the top of the front seat and drops onto my legs.

"Hey hey hey!" I yell, slapping her. "Ow—you could come through the door, you know. Je-sus!"

"Too cold," she says. She starts thumping me, and I fall off the seat and she takes my place and then we start fighting— not for real, of course—and then we're exhausted and then we do some fine singing and then we take pictures of the sky, and I guess maybe a half an hour has gone by when we hear a door slam.

So we sit up—boing, like a couple of prairie dogs—to see. There's Max, and gee, he really does look happy, and there's his girlfriend. She's tall and pretty in that super-healthy way. You know, fresh and glowing. Max has his arm around her and they stop in the middle of the driveway and hug—aww—and then they're kissing, and Frankie and I look at each other, *eeek*, and dive back down again, giggling.

"We're so mature," I say.

"We are!" says Frankie. "We're being respectful."

"They're really going to enjoy having us in the backseat watching them all the way home," I say. "Look! Here's me, being respectful!" I get really close to Frankie's face and bug my eyes out.

But Frankie isn't paying attention. She's—what?—putting her jacket on and getting out of the car. "Franklin!" I say, but she doesn't stop. She's walking right to Max and girlfriend. I mean, they've stopped kissing, but still. Not respectful. Jeez.

The three of them stand in the driveway for a long time, talking. What the hell? Are they discussing the weather? First Frankie talks for a while, with assorted gestures I can't figure out. Max and girlfriend (I will start calling her by her name as soon as I remember it) are nodding and saying occasional words. Why isn't Max telling her to fuck off and get back in the car? Then Max looks at girlfriend and raises his eyebrows. Girlfriend shrugs and smiles and—cute!—pulls his arm around her. Max looks down at her and grins, and then he turns back to Frankie. He's saying something. He's shaking his head. Girlfriend nods. Frankie turns around to look at the car and then turns back to him.

I repeat, What the fuck?

Now Frankie's walking, hard, to the car. She slides in next to me and slams the door shut. "They won't let me do it the way I want," she says grumpily. "They say I have to tell you or it's unethical. Assholes."

I roll my eyes. "That's gripping but I have no idea what you're talking about."

She's not looking at me. "We're four hours and twenty-one minutes away from Sisters, Oregon." I make an involuntary weird noise, which she ignores. "Max and Raina are willing to go but not unless you say you want to." She turns to look at me. "So. You want to?"

Now?

Today?

I open my mouth, but what I say is, "Why would they do this?"

"Who? Max and Raina?" Frankie asks and I nod. "Max owes me, first of all, and second, they kind of want you to meet Sid."

I blink.

Frankie does not consider this an answer. "Char, it's not like life or death."

I nod.

Frankie does not consider this an answer either. "We're not going to leave you up there. We're going to take you to visit him for, like, an hour."

I nod some more.

"You said 'How could it ever happen?' and now it can

happen," says Frankie. There is a not-tiny note of irritation in her voice. "If you're not willing to do this, I might kill you, Char."

I nod again.

"Say something!" she yells.

"I'm thinking," I say, and it's true. Here's what I'm thinking, in chronological order:

1. There is no way this can turn out well. Really, there's no way this can be anything other than awkward and weird. Because why would I go there? What do I want? Isn't it enough that Sid and I talk about interesting things and like each other? Why do I need to see him? Why is it so important to, like, be in his physical presence? That's the question that Sid will probably be asking himself—and that's a freaky one, because physical presence = bodies = (this is really embarrassing to say, but it's the reality) sex or the idea of it. So is my point to go up there and check him out, like to see if he's hot? That's so uncomfortable. It's like I'm inspecting his manhood. Ew. Which by the way he probably doesn't have, because he's probably a little kid. At least thirty-five percent of the fifteen-year-old guy population is a little kid.

2. Because it will be awkward and weird, Sid and I will probably stop being friends. I mean, we'll send a few more texts, sort of pretending that everything's the same and it's great that we met and wasn't it fun, and then it'll just fall away and we won't talk anymore.

3. But is that tragic? Will that ruin my life? I don't know. Maybe this is what *should* happen. I mean, this thing with him is probably just stupid. It's giving me this idea that there's some major destiny for us, when there probably is not. [Here I glance at Frankie, who's watching me, and I think how funny it is that she's doing this to prove that Taking Action Is the Key to Happiness, and what this event will probably prove is that, nah, it really isn't. Forget these brackets, this is part of the same idea: I'm a big liar. I've been doing the romantic daydream thing about Sid for the last couple of months. What a hypocrite! I'm writing a book called Nothing, and at the same time, I'm thinking, If only I could meet Sid, I'd have this *relationship*, tra la, with the birdies singing. Yeah, sure. In some part of my mind, he's been the plot that I tragically can't have because we are tragically separated by five hundred miles. But maybe if I meet him, this will be finished, because I'm pretty fucking sure there is no plot.

4. If there is no plot, what do I do? Am I afraid to lose this dreamy thing with the birdies? Yes. So afraid I won't allow us to meet when we can? What a lame-ass! I should just go up there and meet him and face the fact that it's not going to be some great Romance. Because—

5. It's fake the way it is. Texting. I know this. In a text, you make yourself a certain way. You set things up, you sound good. If you're me, you put up cute pictures of yourself. It's

fake. My mom and dad are right about this (not that I'm going to tell them so): You find out more about people by spending one minute in the same room with them than you do in a year of texting. So my relationship with Sid is fake. (As of now.)

6. Last but really, really not least is that I appreciate Frankie's effort. Okay, so she's being kind of controlling and manipulative (you *are*, Lester), but she's trying to change my worldview because she loves me. She's a good friend. She's not dumping me. I doubted her and I was wrong. I have a really good friend.

7. No, actually, this is the last thing: I'm not really worried about the two noses thing. I doubt he's like, deformed. Still. He might be.

It's also amazing how fast I think all this. Frankie is only just beginning to hold her head and scream when my fingers start texting. *You're home, right?*

Yeah. Why?

Long pause while I try to find the right words. *It seems like I might be driving through Sisters this afternoon. Can I come and say hi?* Send.

I was wrong about number seven. Now I am thinking, What if he has scars, like big creepy ones, on his arms. Oh shit.

What? Is he not going to answer me? Fucking pussy.

But then it's not on me!

Don't answer, don't answer!

Yay! I'm off the—

Pulsing dots.

Pulsing dots.

Pulsing dots.

Yes

That's it? Asshole. I hate him.

Pulsing dots.

Pulsing dots.

Pulsing dots.

Please

Okay. I don't hate him anymore. I don't like him, but I don't hate him, either. He is an acquaintance. I'll drop by and see him, since he's an acquaintance and it's not that far.

"Okay," I say.

"Okay, I want to," Frankie presses.

"Stop being pushy," I say.

"Jesus Christ, first I'm unethical and now I'm pushy!" She really is getting mad. "I'm *helping* you get what you said you couldn't have!"

I reach for her hand and squeeze it. "I know. But you're not me. You can't make me want what you would want. I'm a ledge person. You're a jump person."

Frankie shakes her head. "Loser."

There's a blast of icy cold as the back door opens and slams shut, and then Max and Raina slide in the front. "It's fucking freezing out there!" he squawks. "I thought this was only going to take a minute!"

"Sorry," says Frankie. "Someone was being a pain in the ass."

He turns around to look at her and me. "So?"

"On to Sisters," says Frankie.

"I want to hear it from Charlotte," he says.

"Good luck with that," mutters Frankie kind of bitterly.

"Yitch," I say to her, and then I smile big at Max. "I want to go. It's really nice of you guys to do this, and I'm excited."

Raina turns around, and I see that she's even prettier up close, in that same healthy, glowing way. She has incredible teeth. "This is the most fun I've had all break," she says.

Max turns around and grins at her, and she hits him on the leg. They are having a plot.

How to Figure Out What Percentage of Your Life You're about to Ruin

"'Oregon Welcomes You'," said Frankie, reading the sign at the edge of the road.

"What the hell is that?" asked Charlotte, turning to look.

"I think it was an eagle," said Raina.

"It looked like a rabbit to me," said Frankie.

"Oh great," said Charlotte. "So that's what Oregonians do for fun, dick around with innocent travelers by putting up weird signs." She's nervous, thought Frankie. "They say Oregon welcomes you, and then they gaslight you with eagles that look like rabbits, so you say to yourself, Where are the rabbits? I don't see any rabbits! I must be going insane! And what if you are a rabbit?" She turned to Frankie with wide eyes. "You think you're safe here; you come scampering over the hills, thinking, At last I've found my place on earth and I am a fulfilled rabbit, and then what happens? You get fucking ripped apart by an eagle, that's what!"

"You're nervous, aren't you?" asked Raina.

"Me?" said Charlotte.

"Yes," said Frankie.

"I get nervous before tests," Raina went on. "Fraud complex. Anyway, I do this thing that calms me down—"

"Is it mindfulness?" Charlotte interrupted.

Raina frowned. "No."

"Good," said Frankie. "We're sick of mindfulness."

"It's this calculation thing where I think about how long I'll actually have to pay for it if I screw up."

"What do you mean by pay for it?" asked Charlotte.

"Ah, make up for it, feel bad about it—depends what it is. With a test, I think about how, if I flunk, I'll have to make up the class another semester, and sure, that'll suck, but the point—for me—is that there's no way it's going to set me back more than about six months, right? And then I figure out what fraction of my life that is."

"Lot of math," observed Frankie.

Raina smiled. "Yeah. It got way easier when I turned twenty. Once I figure it out, I realize that six months is only one-fortieth of my life—and getting less every year—and how much do I have to worry about one-fortieth of my life? Not that much." She looked at Charlotte. "It's very comforting."

Charlotte nodded thoughtfully. "Hang on a sec." She looked at Frankie. "How long will I feel bad if this ruins everything between me and Sid?"

Frankie sucked on her lip, thinking. "A month? Maybe two?"

"Make it three," said Charlotte gloomily. "With little bad-feeling islands over the next year or so."

"Okay, let's go with four, to be generous," said Frankie.

"Yeah, let's be generous with my bad feelings," said Charlotte. "Wait." She closed one eye. "So that leaves eight months of the year that I'm okay, right?"

Frankie nodded.

"Which means I've got fourteen years and eight months of okay-ness versus four months of sucky-ness."

"Which means," Raina paused to multiply, ". . . plus eight is one hundred seventy-six months against four months. "

"You're fast," said Frankie.

"I do this a lot. One hundred seventy-six out of one-eighty total. That means"—she closed her eyes—"ninety-seven-plus percent of your life is okay. Only two and a little bit percent is sucky." She opened her eyes. "Doesn't that make you feel better?"

Charlotte nodded. "It does, actually. What's two percent? Almost nothing."

"A rounding error," called Max.

"And the percent gets smaller every year you live," Raina added encouragingly.

"Two percent!" scoffed Charlotte. "Psht! Like two percent even *counts*!"

"She's still nervous," said Frankie to Raina.

Charlotte studied the map on her phone. "Okay, I'm going to redo my eyeliner in Bend," she announced.

"Good plan," said Frankie, also studying her phone.

"I'm not stopping so you can redo your eyeliner," called Max.

"I don't need you to stop," Charlotte called back. "So there." She glanced at Frankie. "Is this what it's like with him around? All this judgment all the time?"

Frankie nodded. "My life is a nightmare."

"Hey!" yelled Max. "Am I driving you two up to Oregon or am I not?"

"Oops. Sorry. You're amazing, Max," said Charlotte. "Give us some more of those great judgments."

"Yeah," called Frankie. "We want to improve ourselves."

"You could stop talking about how you look all the time," said Max. "That'd be an improvement."

Raina stuck her head between the front seats, and she and Frankie and Charlotte made kill-me-now faces at each other.

"And after that, you could stop talking about how people you don't even know look," Max continued. "I mean, who the hell cares about Whatsername Jenner's lips?"

"Okay, we're good now," Frankie said. "That's enough improvement."

"You asked."

There was a silence. Then Charlotte said, "You know, Max, I think it's sort of sad that you don't care about Kylie Jenner's lips. A little bit lacking in empathy. It's like you're saying that we should only care about stuff that's directly related to us, but that's pretty self-absorbed, don't you think?"

"Yeah," Frankie agreed. "When I think about Kylie Jenner and her lips, my world gets a little bigger."

"And my heart gets a little fuller," said Charlotte. "It's like soul collagen!"

They snickered.

"How can we be in Three Rivers?" said Charlotte. She looked at her phone. "We're not supposed to be here yet."

"It's only four hours and twenty minutes if you drive the speed limit," Max said. He looked in his rearview mirror. "Which we're not."

"How long before Sisters?" asked Charlotte.

"Depends on whether we get stuck behind a truck," he said.

"Frankie?" Charlotte searched for her hand.

"Wait, wait, I'm texting Mom," said Frankie. "Again."

Max frowned. "Is she freaking?"

Frankie shook her head. "No. She's fine. We're taking a scenic drive to a restaurant that Raina really likes that's a little farther north."

He laughed. "Good one."

"And we really like Raina—that part's not a lie—and you guys seem really happy—that part's not a lie either—and we're all having lots of fun."

"Good clean fun," Charlotte added.

"And we'll be home pretty late, but Mom shouldn't worry because Raina's going to help drive home," Frankie concluded.

"That part's not a lie, either," said Raina. She looked at Max. "You're tired, huh?"

"Yeah," he said. "I got up early."

"Poor M." Raina touched his shoulder. "We'll take a break in Sisters."

"We need to make the restaurant not a lie, too," he said. "I'm hungry."

● ● ●

With a soft groan, Max pulled into a parking space outside the First Pour Brewpub. Almost before the engine was off, he was out of the car.

"Wow," he said, rubbing his back. "That's a lot of driving."

Slowly Frankie and Charlotte emerged from the car. They exchanged glances.

"Um, Max?" said Frankie.

"What?"

"Uh—we need to go to Sid's," Frankie pointed out.

"I know," he sighed. "I just had to get out of the car for a second." He twisted from side to side, his bones cracking.

"Max!" said Frankie suddenly. "I'll do it."

"You'll do what?"

"I'll drive Char to his house." She held out her hand for the car keys. "I want to."

"Oh, yeah, right," began Charlotte sarcastically. "So we can all end up in jail. They probably still hang people in Sisters, Oregon, for stuff like driving without a—"

Max tossed Frankie the car keys. "Okay."

Raina frowned. "Max?"

"She's fine," he explained. "Really. She's a good driver. And you know, this whole thing was her idea. And she's been ordering everyone around all day long. It's time she walked the walk."

Frankie grinned at him. "Thanks, bruh."

"You're insane!" squawked Charlotte.

"You *are* kind of insane," Raina said. She looked at Frankie's excited face. "But also empowering."

"Also tired and hungry," Max pointed out.

"You're going to let her drive?" yelped Charlotte. "It's dark! She doesn't know where she's going!"

"There's headlights," Frankie said. "And I do know where I'm going because I looked it up. It's not that far."

"It's a mile! At least!"

Raina and Max laughed. "A mile's not far," explained Frankie. "Will you bail me out of jail if I get caught?" she said to her brother.

"Yeah." He looked up and down the empty street. "But I think you're going to be fine."

Frankie tossed the car keys up in the air and caught them. "This is great!"

"Good. Go away," said Max. He put his arm around Raina. "Be back here in exactly ninety minutes. Eight o'clock. If you're late, we're going to get a hotel room and not tell you where it is."

Frankie stuck her tongue out at him. "I don't want to know where it is."

They heard his bones crackle as he turned away toward the restaurant. "Eight o'clock."

For a moment, they stood in the gravelly road, watching

Max and Raina go. Then Frankie turned briskly toward the car. "Okay, then!" she said.

"I can't believe this," muttered Charlotte.

"You want to make a right in eight hundred feet," Charlotte said loudly.

"How soon is eight hundred feet?" Frankie said. She leaned forward to see the farthest reaches of the headlight glow on the pavement.

"Right there! Right here!" cried Charlotte.

Very slowly, Frankie turned right. Very slowly, she drove along a smooth curving road, marked by spare, black trees. Up and up and—

"This is it," said Charlotte.

Frankie pulled with extreme caution to the side of the road. "That only took ten minutes."

"Very small percentage of our lives," muttered Charlotte. She was texting I'm here.

"Okay. Let's go."

"Oh no you don't," said Frankie firmly. "Not me, Char. I did my part. I got you here."

"What're you going to do? Sit out here in the car for eighty minutes?"

"Seventy. We need to leave ten minutes to get back. I'm going to take a nap. That's why I brought the blanket."

Charlotte sighed. "This seems wrong. What if you freeze?"

"Get out. You only have sixty-eight minutes now."

"Oh shit, we'll hardly be able to have sex in sixty-eight minutes," Charlotte said.

"Go!"

"This is stupid."

"Go!"

Taking a deep breath, Charlotte opened the door, stepped out, and disappeared into the darkness.

NOTHING

I feel really weird.

I am about to meet Sid.

I am at Sid's house.

I think I am, anyway. Because I can't see a damn thing. It's completely pitch-black.

Then my eyes figure it out, and I begin to see a path under some trees. I take very slow and careful steps. One. Two. Three. I am probably going to be eaten by a bear before I get to the door. Four. Oh! A house suddenly appears below me, lights shining from its windows—and now, the front door opens and makes a rectangle of gold. Good, good, I'm not going to be eaten by a bear, but my stomach is now doing some strange stuff, so I still might die before I get there. And now, a black figure appears in the gold rectangle. Okay! I know one thing about Sid! He's not obese! Yay for me! Well, really, yay for him. Not that I'm fattist or anything.

"Hi," he calls.

"Hi," I call back. "I'm trying not to die on your path."

"Why would you die?" He sounds worried. Oh shit, we've started off with him not understanding what I mean, we're fucked, I've upset him, he has no sense of humor, oh god oh god oh god, I want to leave right now.

"Bears," I say. "I was thinking about bears." I sound like an idiot. But now I am in front of his door. Now I am seeing him for the first time.

One nose.

No acne. Not disfiguring acne, anyway. I mean, not perfect, but in the range. Like me.

My eyes fall to his arms. He's wearing a sweatshirt-y thing. So weird scars are still an option.

I realize, suddenly, that he's looking at me looking at him. Oh my god, this is so fucking awkward.

"Hi," I say, and it comes out in a long sighing breath. This is horrible. I hate my life.

"Hi," he says, and I think he sounds stiff. But he opens the door and says, "Come on in."

I step through the door and I'm so nervous that I'm sweating, even though it's really cold, and I start thinking about how I look when I sweat, and before I can stop myself, I'm doing this free-association thing I do when I'm freaking. "So, like, what's with the sign Oregon Welcomes You? Is it a rabbit or an eagle? Sorry. Um, hi. You're not"—oh sweet Jesus, I stop myself before I say "white," which is what I was about to say, because I'm thinking of his snow-selfie, but thank god I don't say it, because he's not white, he's something else—"snow," I say really quick.

He looks at me, kind of frowning in confusion. "I'm not snow?"

I could completely lose it here. I could also, I realize, cat. I mean, I could tear out the front door, up the path, and into the car, and peel away at a hundred miles an hour. This is what I want to do. I want it bad. There's only one thing that keeps me in Sid's front hall: explaining to Max and Raina that they drove all that way for nothing. Maybe I could lie.

Okay, there's another thing that keeps me here. I am not being myself. This is probably also true about Sid. I know him. He's my friend. Was my friend.

I try really really hard to stop freaking out, and I say, semi-normally, "You know, your selfie, the one you made with snow."

His face clears a little. "Oh. That. Right. Um, you wanna meet my mom?"

"Sure! Great!" I say, super-enthusiastically, like that's why I came. And the truth is, I am dying to meet his mom, because she will do that grown-up small-talk thing, which would be paradise compared to this.

So he walks down the hall, a little ahead of me, which helps, because he's not looking at me, and we go into the kitchen, where his mom is listening to one of those "Well, tell me, Jim, how do you see this playing out in Geneva?"–type radio shows and chopping vegetables. She smiles really nicely at me, which makes me feel better, and says, "Hi, Charlotte, I'm Jaya. It's so nice you could come by."

Oh, I love you, lady. I have just "come by." No commitment. No pressure. And she has a nice voice, too. She is my favorite person.

"Hi, Jaya," I say. "Thanks."

"Are you hungry?" She waves a radish at me. "Veggies and dip." There's a little plate set out on the counter.

"Uh. Sure. That's great." I sort of sidle toward the counter, but then I either have to reach around her or else walk toward Sid, which I don't think I can do. I don't think I can do either thing. I halt in mid-sidle.

"There's chairs over here," says Sid, gesturing stiffly at the other side of the counter.

Oh. Like barstools. Gotcha. I try to look like a person who lives in a place with furniture. "Right," I say, and sidle around the counter and sit down.

"How long are you going to visit Sisters?" Jaya asks, still working on her radish.

I look at the clock. "Fifty-three more minutes," I say.

Jaya laughs. "Short visit."

Sid says, "Fifty-three minutes is more than enough for Sisters."

Jaya makes a face at him. "Now. There's lots to see here."

"Fifty-four minutes," he says. "Tops."

"Sid," she says in that warning-mom way.

"Um, I thought it was a majestic natural wonderland," I say. "What I could see of it, anyway."

Sid looks sideways at me and for the first time since I walked in, we're friends. "Majestic natural wonderland?"

"For sure," I say, feeling a little better. "I saw a snowy crag."

"Oh, yeah!" he says, and now he's even smiling a little. "We call that the Snowy Crag."

I kind of, you know, giggle, and he falls silent. I also fall silent. Silence falls. I go back to hating my life. No. I think I'll hate him for a while. Why the hell isn't he helping me more? Why is he being so quiet and un-fucking-friendly.

Asshole.

"Why don't you show Charlotte the studio?" says Jaya.

There is now a little bit of desperation in her nice voice.

"You want to see the studio?" says Sid in an un-fucking-friendly way.

"Sure," I say, also in an un-fucking-friendly way.

He slips off his barstool and moves toward another hall. Then he stops and looks over his shoulder at me. "It's this way."

I'm tired. I get off my barstool and follow him. We are walking down another hall and—what?—out a door, and now we're outside in the cold and dark.

"There aren't any bears," he says ahead of me

"I know," I say quickly. "I was kidding."

"Oh."

Asshole.

"There are wolverines, though," he says.

"But unlike bears, wolverines won't kill you," I say, admittedly stupidly, because I've just said that I never thought there *were* bears. Ugh. I hate my life.

"Sure they will," Sid says.

"Nah. You don't know," I say. "Wolverines are little."

"You're saying I don't know wolverines?" says Sid, and I think he's joking, but I don't know.

"Yeah," I say. "That's what I'm saying."

"And you do?" We have arrived at some sort of building, and he is fumbling in his pocket.

I really have no idea if he's joking. I don't even know this guy. I don't know whether he jokes without showing it in his voice. But I keep going. "Hello? I know wolverines like the back of my hand."

"Tell me a wolverine fact," he says, a little absently because he's unlocking the door.

"Wolverines are closely related to the elephant," I say.

"Psht. There's a little step," he says, and turns on a light.

I step inside, not tripping. Yay, Charlotte. I look up and— wow. It's like a real artist's studio. There's an enormous table on one side with paint and pencils and brushes on it and one of those file-drawer things for art and an easel in the middle and—get this—a wire cage setup for storing paintings. Which is filled with paintings.

"Wow," I say, looking at the wire cage. "You did all those?"

"No," he says. "Those're my dad's."

"He's a painter?"

"Yeah."

"Like, that's his job?"

"He teaches, too."

"Wow. That's pretty cool."

"He's a dick."

Oh. What am I supposed to say here? "How come?"

He glances at me and shakes his head. "He just is. He dumped my mom for one of his students last year."

Huh. The secret drama of Sid. Never before mentioned.

Because we just text about fun stuff. "You're right. That's pretty dickish."

He turns to look at the wire cage. "I tried to get Mom to burn them, but she wouldn't."

"She doesn't seem like a person who would burn paintings," I say. Am I? I'd like to be. But I'm probably not. "Maybe you could do something less noticeable," I say.

"Like what?"

"I don't know. You could add, like, a little tiny stick man on all of them."

He smiles. "He'd kill me." He gives a half-laugh. "It'd feel really good, though." He turns to look at the wire cage again.

And now, for, like, a *second*, I have a chance to look at him without him knowing. And? And, I don't know. Really. I don't. Here's what I see: He's not a little boy. He's not a man, either. He's, like, a teenage guy. Taller than me, but not that much. Not a twig guy, but sure as heck not yoked, either. His wrists might be smaller than mine. Like I said, he's something other than white, but I don't know what it is. He's got really dark brown eyes. Long eyelashes. And get this: he's got black hair in a ponytail that's, like, down to his waist.

I don't know what I think of this.

I mean, I don't know what I think of him, attractiveness-wise.

I mean, I don't know whether I consider him a prospect anymore.

To make myself clear, I'm not saying "I don't know" and meaning yuck. I mean I really don't know. And this is making me think there is something wrong with me.

Seriously wrong with me.

Here is the truth: I don't know what I think of him because I don't know any guy who wears his hair like that.

That is so fucked I can't stand it.

I have no individuality. I'm a prisoner of my context, just like Ms. Heath says. I'm a sheep.

Oh. My. God. What a loser I am.

What a tap.

I hate people like me.

My second is over. He turns back to me and shrugs.

I am such a tap that I feel sorry for him, just in case he thought, like I did, that we were a possible thing and now there's no chemistry for the fucked-up reason that I can't figure out whether I'm into him because I don't know any guys with hair like his. So I say, "You could just do it on one."

He laughs, in a really nice way. "Okay. You pressured me into it."

Then he goes over to the cage and pulls out this medium-sized painting and lays it on the enormous table.

"How come you're not using the easel?" I ask.

He glances at the easel. "That's his. I do my stuff here."

"The painting's his, too," I point out.

"Hey," he says, but not mad or anything. I go over and lean against the table, watching him. He's got a million jars full of pencils and pens and stuff. I never knew anyone who had this kind of art stuff. He starts rattling around in a jar and pulls out a little brush. Without even looking, like he already knows which one he wants. I can tell this is what he does. You know, in life.

"So, you're, like, really an artist, aren't you?"

He's yanking out a drawer with paint in it, but he glances up at me. "I do other stuff, too."

"Like what?"

"Like"—he kind of sighs—"I used to play soccer and all that."

I nod, watching him. He's putting a little blob of white and a littler blob of black on a plastic tray. "Where are you going to put it?"

He looks at the painting. It's this crazy mashed-up red dog with a giant orange bone behind it. I guess the bone is chasing the dog. It's not the greatest painting.

"On the dog," he says. "On its nose, so it'll stand out." He tilts his head to one side, and then mixes some of the white and some of the black into light gray. He does it really quickly.

"So you paint, too?"

He shakes his head. "Not really. I'm more into drawing. Also"—he paints a few strokes on a piece of paper and puts a tiny bit more white into the gray—"photography and"—he bends way over the painting and quickly paints a small, whitish stick guy, just zip-zip, like it's the easiest thing in the world. He straightens up—"computer graphics. And sometimes this other stuff, installation-y stuff. I don't know what you'd call it." He looks at what he's done and smiles. "That felt really good. I hate this picture."

I look at his stick figure. When I make a stick figure, it's a circle on top of a cross with little legs. Sid's stick figure looks like a person. Its arms and legs have muscles. It's got hair. I'm impressed and all, but I'm also jealous—he can actually *make* stuff. I wish I could do that.

"Can I see some of your other stuff?" I ask, hoping that's an okay question.

"Oh. Yeah." He looks around. "There's some drawings in here." He gets up and opens one of the big, flat drawers.

"I love my porcupine," I say, remembering it suddenly.

He nods. "You don't know shit about animals."

I laugh. "Fuck you, I'm an animologist." The drawing on top is of a dead fish on a counter. "For instance, that's a dead fish," I say, and then add, "also a really good drawing." I don't want him to think I'm not appreciating his art. He leans over to pick up the picture, and his ponytail falls over his shoulder, and he does this shoulder-swing move that flops it back without him touching it. I look quickly back at the drawer, where there is an amazing picture of some rocks. It must be colored pencil, but I don't see how he made it so perfect. I'd say it looks real, but it actually looks better than that. Under that, there's one of a cloth something, crumpled on a floor. "Whoa," I mutter. "That's amazing."

"That's toilet paper," he says.

"Art you can make with common household objects," I mutter, but inside I'm thinking: Wow. He's an *artist*. Like for real. He's not just waiting around to get old before he gets good at something. He's already doing it. "I can't believe you do all this stuff," I say.

"Yeah," he says. Whatever that means.

My phone has a seizure. *Time's up*, says Frankie. She's right, too.

"I have to go," I say.

He nods. "Okay."

Fuck! We have returned to the land of incredible awkwardness again. Fuck!

"Hah," I say, in a deeply stupid fashion. "I—um—I'm glad we got to meet finally." I am such a gler. I sound like I'm trying to be a grown-up, like I don't like him. Help me, God.

"Me, too," he says, also grown-upishly.

"I wish I could see more of your stuff."

He shrugs. "Maybe next time."

I nod. "Um. Should I go back through the house or . . . ?"

He looks like he doesn't know what I'm talking about. Then, "Oh! No. There's a path. I'll take you. It's pretty dark."

I cannot think of one damn thing to say, so we leave the studio in silence and start crunching up a path. It's totally dark, and I am hamster-braining, trying to think of something to say, and you know what I come up with? "You're leading me into a wolverine nest to kill me, right?" Oh so brilliant.

All he says is "Yeah."

I can't see *anything* and I am feeling more terrible every second because

(a) we probably won't be friends anymore after this,

(b) I'm such a loser I can't figure out whether I'm attracted to his *hair*,

(c) and I miss him already.

I've fucked this up for nothing. I should never have let Frankie bring me here. "I'm sorry," I blurt.

"About what?" he says in the darkness.

"I shouldn't have come. I'm sorry. It's a fuckup." He stops and I kind of ram into him, which makes him almost fall over. Like I said, he's not that much bigger than I am. "I'll miss you if you don't want to text anymore," I say. Which I'm sort of proud that I had the guts to say.

"I still want to," he says. And that's all. It's not like a tender romantic moment where he takes my hand in his (although that would have been *nice*, considering how dark it was). We just walk to the car and I open the door.

Frankie leans toward me. "Shake your ass, girl. They're going to get a hotel room in six minutes. Oh!"

"This is Sid." I slice my hands back and forth. "This is Frankie."

"Hi Frankie," he says.

"Hi Sid," she says. "My brother's going to get a hotel room with his girlfriend and not tell us where it is if we don't get back to town in six minutes," she explains.

"Oh," he says, confusedly.

"So we'd better go," I say. Pause. "Um—thanks."

And then there's this tiny—and of course, because that's our theme, awkward—moment where he reaches out and squeezes my lower arm. Maybe he was aiming for my hand. And I kind of put my hand on his shoulder and tighten it a little. We accept the hug we think we deserve. Fuck me.

I get in the car and Frankie starts it. I buzz down the window. "Bye," I say.

"Bye." He leans down and his ponytail is dangling over his shoulder again. I kind of want to pull it, but I don't. "Thanks for coming."

And Frankie drives away.

Funny, It Seems Just Like the Old Year

"This is called a three-point turn," Frankie said into the darkness. She looked in her rearview mirror. She put the car into reverse. She looked into her rearview mirror again. She touched the accelerator carefully. So carefully that nothing happened. A little harder. The car went backward. She stopped and put the car into drive. Gently, she pressed the accelerator. "Very good," she said. "Proceed to da route."

Silence.

Frankie drove.

Silence.

Frankie pulled over to the side of the road. "Are you okay?"

"Why'd you pull over?"

At least her voice was normal. "Because I'm not a good enough driver to look at you and drive at the same time," Frankie explained. "I had to pull over to look at you. I can't really see you, though."

"We're going to be late," Charlotte warned.

"Are you okay?"

"Yeah."

"Okay." Frankie pulled back onto the road and drove, peering over the steering wheel into the darkness.

"Left here," said Charlotte quietly.

"'Kay."

Back at First Pour, Max and Raina were already waiting on the curb. Max stepped forward to open Charlotte's door. "'Bout time."

"We're, like, two minutes late," protested Frankie, stepping out. "I did it!"

"You didn't even get arrested and hanged," said Raina, taking her place.

Max handed a bag over the seat. "We got you guys some pizza."

"Wow. Thanks," said Frankie. "Smells great."

When everyone was settled, Raina turned around. "How was it?" she asked Charlotte.

Charlotte looked up. "It was—interesting." Only Frankie knew she was making an effort. "Thanks, you guys, for doing it. Really."

"Long drive ahead," said Max, yawning.

"Everyone sleep," said Raina. She patted Max on the head. "I've got this."

"I'm not going to sleep," he said. "I'm going to keep you company."

"You know what I think?" she said. "I think guys find it emasculating to sleep in a car while a woman drives."

"Theory alert," he said.

Raina laughed. "Go to sleep."

But Frankie didn't, not for a long time. And neither did Charlotte. Her eyes were closed, but Frankie could tell she wasn't sleeping.

It was 4:15 in the morning when they finally dropped into the beds in Frankie's room. "Any later, and we would have run into Mom and Dad getting up," said Frankie, mashing her pillow into the perfect shape.

"Uh," mumbled Charlotte. "I should wash my face."

"Tomorrow. We'll do all that stuff tomorrow."

"Tomorrow is today," sighed Charlotte.

"No more Happy New Year," said Frankie.

"Mm," said Charlotte. "Same to you."

●　●　●

When they woke up the next morning, it was hardly morning anymore, and when they stumbled out to the kitchen, Frankie's mom did a lot of clucking about how late they'd slept and how they needed protein immediately, while Charlotte just sat quietly at the breakfast table. Maybe she's sleepy, Frankie thought. We'll talk later. But after breakfast/lunch, Charlotte's mom came clumping across the porch and Frankie could tell Charlotte was glad—although maybe she was just glad because she liked her mom—and even when she was hugging Frankie and telling her how fun it had been, Frankie knew she was feeling weird. We'll talk later, thought Frankie. But then Frankie's dad came into the kitchen and stared mournfully at Frankie for a long time until he couldn't stand it anymore and had to point out that school started again in two days—as if Frankie didn't know that—and then ask in an aggravatingly neutral way how much homework she still had to do. Frankie decided that her best bet was to act like a sullen teenager and huff off to her room, but once she was there, she looked in her backpack and noticed that she really did have a lot of social studies reading and a whole set of problems for chem, not to mention un peu de français pour Monsieur Vargas, who could be très sarcastic if you didn't faire your devoirs. So Frankie nobly got down to it and also nobly did chem first and discovered that she was totally fucked, which meant she had to call Gaby, who was really good at math, which in turn meant she had to hear all about New Year's and Alex, who was acting weird and didn't even really talk to Gaby on New Year's, not that Gaby cared *that* much, because hot neighbor Jason was in town, and Gaby had always had a thing for him, and he asked her over on New Year's, which Gaby couldn't do because she was with Alex, but now she regretted it. Finally they got around to chem and Gaby explained the whole thing twice, and Frankie was pretty sure she had it, which it turned out she did, even though it took her the whole rest of the afternoon to finish it, not that that was saying much. Right when Frankie was about to text Charlotte, her mom called, "Dinner!" at which point Max and Raina appeared—for the first time that day—and had dinner with them, which was much more fun than usual, because Raina was a big talker and asked Frankie's dad a lot of personal questions, which you could tell he loved and which revealed some pretty surprising stuff about him. Frankie and Max exchanged secret smiles, and she could see that he was proud that his girlfriend was so cool and fun, and Frankie was glad for him. By the time they were done it was almost nine, and when Frankie texted Charlotte, she didn't text back, at least not for the next half hour and that was when, weirdly, Frankie fell asleep.

So it wasn't until the next day, the last day of break, that

Frankie texted *Want to meet up at Canyon?*

KK. Noony's here but she's got to slide. Half hour?

Yag cu

"I can't believe no one stole it," Frankie said, looking at the little Christmas tree.

"I can. It's pretty ugly," said Charlotte. She sat down next to it and flicked a branch. Needles fell. "The ugly little Christmas tree that outlived all the pretty Christmas trees." She narrowed her eyes into slits and looked suspiciously at Frankie. "Outlived—or murdered?"

"The shitty little Christmas tree," said Frankie, settling in a curve of the rock. "So."

"So," said Charlotte, "I know what you're about to ask."

Frankie nodded. "So. Answer."

"What was it like with Sid?"

Frankie nodded.

Charlotte shuddered. "It was incredibly awkward. Unbelievably awkward. Half the time, I wished one of us would just die."

"No."

"Yes. Then, probably another twenty-five percent of the time, I spent wanting to run out the door and jump in the car and leave."

"Twenty-five percent?"

"Yeah, and then there was about another twenty percent where I was busy hating myself."

"Why?"

"Because I couldn't figure out whether his hair was hot."

Frankie blinked. "What?"

"Did you see his hair?"

Frankie shook her head.

"It was in a ponytail. Down to his waist."

Frankie nodded. "Okay."

"I didn't know what—like, I don't know any guys with hair like that—I didn't know whether I liked it."

Frankie frowned with concentration. "I'm not getting this. The problem is—?"

"I'm a sheep. I really, honestly didn't know what I thought. It was disgusting."

"His hair?"

"No! Me. I'm a loser."

"Help me here, girl," said Frankie, baffled. "You did or didn't like his hair?"

"No!" yelled Charlotte. "I didn't know whether I liked his hair. Because I'd never seen a guy with hair like that before. Get it? I'm, like, incapable of having an individual experience. I don't have my own opinion! I just want what everyone else wants." She put her hands over her eyes. "Ugh. That's so fucked." She pulled her hands away and glared accusingly at Frankie. "You're not like this."

"I'm not?"

"No. You know your dress? Your new one?"

"Yeah."

"When I first saw it on you, it was just like, Does Not Compute, because nobody wears that kind of dress. I thought: That's not a dress for a kid, so I didn't even consider it. I didn't even really see it. It was just Not Us. But you knew you looked great. You knew you wanted it. You're not a sheep. That's what I'm talking about."

Frankie nodded slowly. She was sort of getting it. "So, what I'm hearing—"

"Ooh, baby!" Charlotte giggled. "You are rocking that nonviolent communication!"

"Shut up," Frankie said. "What I'm hearing is that you're disappointed in yourself because you didn't know instantly if you liked Sid's hair."

"Not just instantly. I still don't know," said Charlotte. "Not that it really matters, because I probably won't see him again."

"Wait," said Frankie. She was thinking. "Not to sound like a mom or anything, but if you're noticing it, I think it means you're changing."

Charlotte rolled her eyes. "Oh that's so beautiful. Today I became a woman."

"No, listen. You wouldn't have noticed this if you weren't starting to think something different. I mean, if you weren't beginning to get more independent-minded, you would have looked at his hair and thought Does Not Compute, like you said about the dress. But you noticed it. You're on the fence. Which means you're probably changing."

"Maybe," said Charlotte grudgingly. "I—" she stopped.

"You what?" urged Frankie.

"I hope I am. I don't want to be a sheep. I want to have my own opinions."

Frankie nodded. "About guys' hair."

Charlotte shook her head. "About other stuff, too. I mean, I thought it would be easier this way. You know, accept the things you cannot change. But I think I got too accepting. You end up being a sheep."

Frankie leaned back against the rock. "Yeah, you're for sure about to change or you wouldn't see any of this." She smiled loftily. "The thing is, maybe you're just a little developmentally backward and immature. Probably a little bit slow. Whereas I am amazingly mature and"—she snapped—"*legend* for independent thinking."

"That's not what you're legend for."

They laughed and then watched the clouds in silence for a few moments.

"Wait," said Frankie. "What about the other five percent?"

Charlotte snickered. "Frankie does math!"

"Shut up. What?"

Charlotte closed her eyes. "The other five percent was nice. Maybe even more than five percent. Like, possibly eight percent. I mean, he's pretty cool, as a person. We went to his studio—I guess it's really his dad's, but his dad bailed on his mom last year—and it was amazing. Sid showed me some of his drawings and he painted a stick figure on one of his dad's paintings and I could see—"

"Wait," interrupted Frankie. "He painted on one of his dad's paintings?"

Charlotte opened her eyes. "Yeah. I told him to. I mean, I suggested it. He wanted to burn all his dad's paintings, but his mom wouldn't go for it, so I suggested that he do something more subtle. So he painted a stick guy. But my point is that it was amazing, the way it was so easy for him. It was just—natural. You can just tell he's been doing stuff like that his whole life. I was jealous."

"Did you guys talk about, um"—Frankie tried to find the word—"what's been going on with you?"

Charlotte grinned at her. "Did we talk about us, you mean? No. I said, right at the end, when I was feeling really bad— which, let me be clear, I was, most of the time—that I was sorry I'd come and I'd miss him if we stopped texting."

Frankie nodded, impressed. "What'd he say?"

"He said he didn't want to stop texting."

Frankie nodded, impressed again. "So? That's good."

"Except we haven't."

Frankie's face fell. "Why not?"

"I guess I was waiting for him," Charlotte admitted. "I mean, I went up there! He should text me."

Frankie rolled her eyes. "Look. You went up there, but he's probably thinking, She hated me, she thinks I'm gross and stupid and ugly."

"I don't!" yelped Charlotte.

"Well, don't be mean, then. Text the poor guy."

"Why can't he text me?" Charlotte said, taking out her phone.

"I just said why."

Charlotte looked at her phone. "What should I say?"

Frankie rolled her eyes again. "I'm having a really hard time because I can't decide if your hair is hot."

"So helpful. Did you see him at all?"

"Just a little. Really big dark eyes."

"Yeah. I like that," said Charlotte, half to herself.

"Yeah. Me too," said Frankie.

Charlotte shot her a sideways look. "Zack?"

"Oh yeah. Gorgeous."

"I still can't believe that happened to you."

Frankie giggled. "Me neither. It was great." She frowned at

Charlotte. "Stop trying to distract me. Shut up and text."

"Just trying to be a good friend here," said Charlotte lightly. She looked down at her phone again. "I liked his wrists, too."

"I didn't see them. Text."

Charlotte's fingers skittered over the glass. She stopped. She backspaced. She paused. Skittering fingers. Backspace. Pause. "This is hard," she muttered.

"Just tell him the truth," said Frankie.

"What's the truth? Who the hell knows?" Charlotte grumbled. She sighed heavily and began again, her fingers moving much more slowly.

Okay so there wasn't any real reason why I needed to see you and I know it was super-tense but if I hadn't come I wouldn't have seen you do that painting and that was amazing.

Pause.

Pulsing dots.

The stick figure? Not amazing

Charlotte let out a gusting breath. "He hates me."

Frankie read over her shoulder. "Well. Not exactly friendly, but keep going. He might just need help."

Charlotte took a breath.

I don't mean the stick figure. I mean watching you do it. I didn't know that about you

What didn't you know?

"See? Better," said Frankie.

That you do art so easily

Oh. Yeah. I guess

"Kind of dry," said Frankie, wincing.

"Kind of dry? Dry as hell. He's a withholding asshole," said Charlotte. "I'm not answering." She looked at Frankie. "So I'll be bummed for two-point-three percent of my life. I can deal."

"There sure is a lot of math in these conversations," said Frankie. "But okay. Two-point-three percent—that's nothing!"

Charlotte nodded—and looked at her phone.

Frankie tried for some distraction. "Speaking of Raina, she and Max had dinner with us last night, and you want to know what I found out about my dad?" Charlotte nodded. "He ran away from home when he was fourteen!"

"Tom did?" Charlotte said, surprised. "He seems so law-abiding. How come?"

"He was mad at his dad."

Charlotte's phone twitched.

You there?

"I'm not answering," said Charlotte. "What was he mad about?"

"He was pissed because his dad called him cautious." Frankie laughed. "He wanted to prove him wrong." Charlotte was looking at her phone. "Answer," advised Frankie.

Yeah

Why didn't you answer?

B/c you seemed like a withholding asshole

"Jesus," breathed Frankie.

Okaaay

I was being nice

Pulsing dots.

Pulsing dots.

Pulsing dots.

Blank.

Blank.

Pulsing dots.

Pulsing dots.

Pulsing dots.

Blank.

Blank.

"See? Typical guy," began Charlotte. "You call them on their shit and they freak out and won't talk to you—"

Her phone rang. She raised an eyebrow at Frankie and accepted. "Hello?"

"Hi. It's Sid," he said unnecessarily.

"Yeah. Got that," she said.

"I'm sorry I seemed like a withholding asshole," he said. "I have no idea what you're talking about but I'm still sorry."

"Fine," Charlotte snapped. "Whatever."

"Okay." There was a silence. "Charlotte?"

"Yes, Sid?"

"I saw a video of a wolverine eating a moose."

Charlotte began to smile. "An already-dead moose?"

"No. A live moose. He killed it and ate it."

"Can they jump or something? I mean, a moose is a lot taller than a wolverine."

Frankie held her head in a silent scream of exasperation.

"I'll send you the link."

"Okay."

"I'm trying to help with your animal problem."

"Thanks, but I'm an animal genius. Animals, animals, animals, twenty-four seven."

He laughed. "Sorry I was a withholding asshole."

"Good."

"Bye."

"Bye."

"You should be in your seats, boys and girls," said Miss Mathers the next afternoon.

"Boney girl! How's it hangin'?" Chris slid past Frankie and dropped into his desk.

"Great," she muttered back. "Fifty-four minutes of English. What could possibly be bad?"

He snickered and fist-bumped the other Chris on the head. "My man Chris!"

"Bruh!"

"Lou-*aye!*"

"Hi, Chris," said Luis nervously.

"Boys," warned Miss Mathers.

Indulgently they quieted and trained their eyes on their teacher. "I hope you all had a restful holiday." Miss Mathers looked around the classroom and received some depressed nodding. "Because we have a great deal to achieve in the coming weeks, including some rather *intensive* reading." She bulged her eyes at them. "Now. What I mean by *intensive* reading is not a matter of page length. No. I'm talking about content. Our next book deals with subjects that are—that *will*—require your maturity and sensitivity, and I wish to make very clear"—furrowed brow—"that disrespect will not be accepted. We will be establishing—and of course, *maintaining*—an atmosphere of tolerance, respect, and maturity. Am I making myself understood, students?"

"Sure, Miss Mathers," said Josh.

"I dunno, Miss M," said Chris. "Sometimes I'm just intolerant and I can't help it."

"Chris," said Miss Mathers sternly. "That's enough. Now. We will not be passing out books today. Today we will be doing important *pre-reading* self-exploration."

"Self-exploration?" whispered the other Chris. "That's foul!"

Miss Mathers ignored the ensuing spasm of giggles. "Students, take out a piece of paper—yes, paper, not your computers—and a pen."

Sighing, Frankie complied. After a long period of shuffling and complaining, a slight majority of students had paper in front of them, and Miss Mathers continued. "Now, do not write your name at the top of your paper. This is to be entirely personal and anonymous unless you choose to share it. Now. The assignment is to write down three things that no one in this class would know about you unless you told them."

Blank faces.

"You mean like, secrets?" asked Tara.

"Not necessarily secrets, though secrets may be included. But simply things that are not apparent to your classmates. Three things about who you *are*. Each of your items must begin with the words, 'What you don't know about me is.' Miss Mathers looked around the classroom, clearly persuaded that her students could not help but be thrilled by this opportunity to reveal their innermost selves.

"I don't really get it," said Davindra.

Miss Mathers's face hardened. "I will help you individually, Davindra."

"I don't get it either," said a girl named Suzette, whom Frankie considered to be one of the dumbest people in the entire world.

While Miss Mathers explained the assignment five or six more times, Frankie looked down at her paper. Completely anonymous? Yeah, right. No way was she writing down anything important.

"1. What you don't know about me is—"

She paused. What?

Nothing. I have no secrets because nothing ever happens to me.

Frankie chewed on her pen. She looked at the back of Chris's head. What you don't know about me is that I got together with that guy over there during break. Though—now that she thought about it—Chris knew, which disqualified it as an item.

She tried to think of something better. Christmas? What you don't know about me is I got this fabulous dress for Christmas and I look amazing in it.

Couldn't really put that down.

What you don't know about me is that on New Year's I saved my brother's relationship with his girlfriend. That was a pretty good thing, she thought. And then I got them to drive Charlotte to Oregon to meet Sid. Less good. Or maybe just Outcome Unknown. Still. I was responsible for a lot of relationship development over Christmas break. Thank you, Frankie. I might be a little bossy, though.

Oh! What you don't know about me is that I drove a car without a license. Oh yeah, that's a good one. Call the cops. Ruin my life.

What you don't know about me is—dang if I know.

Concentrate.

What you don't know about me is that this man I'd never seen before in my life kissed me.

Nah. Sounds good, but that's not why I was so happy.

What you don't know about me is that this man looked at me and saw something that blew him away.

Nah, that's not it, either.

What you don't know about me is that I had a moment that was completely separate from the rest of my life.

Closer.

Like I'm going to write any of that. Miss Mathers would call CPS.

Frankie looked around the classroom, seeking inspiration. What you don't know about me is that I know this crap is going to be over soon.

She looked at the clock. Yow. Class was going to be over soon, too. Quickly, she wrote

1. What you don't know about me is that I'm allergic to bell peppers.

2. What you don't know about me is that I'm the youngest of five children.

3. What you don't know about me is that—Frankie decided to throw Miss Mathers a self-exploratory bone—according to my friend Charlotte, I'm a jump person, not a ledge person.

NOTHING

(This is an epilogue.
I never understood
why books
have them, but now
I do.)

Frankie looks up from my laptop. "We suck."

"Told you," I say. I wait for her to say something else, but she doesn't. Hello? The author could use some love here. "Ahem!" I cough.

"What?"

I glare at her. "The author is feeling unappreciated."

Frankie peers at me. Then she gets it. "Oh. Oh, it's great—I mean, you are really a good writer and it's really funny." She nods vigorously.

I find this less than satisfactory. "Feh."

Frankie tries again. "Okay, here's another thing—I think

it's amazing that you can make us sound the way we really do. You did what you said you were going to do, and it's great. It's a searing document about how boring our lives are. A grown-up might freak about the swearing and drugs and stuff, but really, it shows that we're model citizens, most of the time."

Better, but still. I shake my head.

"Jeez. Authors are a pain in the ass. How about this? You made something. And it's really good. You created something. You're, like, a real writer."

That's more like it. I did make something. I think about this for a second—I made something. Like an artist. Like Sid. I can see why a person might want to do this, you know, as a calling. Maybe I'll be a writer instead of a spy. I nod graciously. "Thanks." Pause. "Think I should change Eden's name?"

Frankie thinks about it for a minute and then shakes her head. "She won't read it. You're not going to turn it in until you're a senior, are you?"

"I don't know if I'm ever going to turn it in."

She raises her eyebrows. "What? I thought that was the point. I thought it was your senior project."

I shrug. "First of all, it's kind of personal, and second, I'm hoping something better will happen between now and senior year that I can write about."

"Jesus, I hope so," she says. "I'm hoping that all the stuff in here is just the introduction to some incredible thing that's going to happen next year."

"Probably not," I say. "Sorry to crush your hopes and dreams."

"I know." She looks down at my computer. "Couldn't you add in something exciting? You know, put in just one untrue good thing?"

"And then there was a tsunami and as they clung to a palm tree, they realized that they had always loved each other, but at the moment their lips met, Charlotte lost her grip on the tree and was dragged out into the ocean, and the last thing Frankie saw was her butt."

Frankie laughs. "Yeah, like that. I was thinking something like we go to Paris and meet hot guys, but yours is fine, too."

"The point is to tell the truth."

"Yeah, but you know, we're in process here," she says. "We're probably destined for exciting events. You could just slip one in before it actually happens."

"Who's the author here?" I huff. "I'm leaving it the way it is."

"Fine. Have it your way. But it's kind of bumming me out."

"Too bad," I say. I hold out my hand and she passes me my computer. "Nothing rules."

Frankie groans.

● ● ●

Okay. So.

I really *was* right, you know. Nothing did happen. The history of Charlotte's sophomore year: Nothing, nothing, nothing, nothing, zits, nothing, nothing, nothing, repeat. That is the genuine honest-to-god truth.

Except that about seven months later, something did sort of happen. And in honor of Frankie, I'm going to add it in. [Okay, Frankie? Are you happy now?]

Not that it's a big deal. It's not. But it is what I guess you could call an outcome. A related event.

Somewhere in the middle of July—can't remember exactly when; a few days after Frankie and Noony and I got back from this camp we've been going to for a hundred years, but now we're CITs—I got a text from Sid saying he's coming into town. Because—another previously unmentioned Sid fact—his aunt lives in San Francisco, and he and his mom are coming to visit her for a day and a half before they fly to New York for some damn thing. So. What? I freak out a little because after the Sisters of Living Hell, it took us, like, a month to get normal again. But we did get normal, and even a tiny bit more, ah, personal. Not as in sexting, you pervs, as in

Help, my mom's crying what shd I do?

Hug her, you tap

Okay

Anyway, after I freak out a little, I do some major consulting with Frankie and we decide that the best way to avoid the Sisters of Living Hell is to keep moving. So I put together an astoundingly—if I do say so myself—fun day, where we go all over the place and see all the things I think an artist guy would like to see (that we can get to by bus and walking). We go to the top of the university tower; we go see these weird dinosaur heads they have in the science building; I show him a house shaped like an orange, which he thinks is really funny; we eat at Flats, which is a crepe place; and we go to a store that's famous around here for selling creepy stuff.

After that, I'm thinking that he's going to say he has to go (because doesn't he have to see his aunt? He's only here for a day and a half!). But he doesn't. He says, "Show me the rock where you take all those pictures."

So I take him up to Canyon. And by this time, it's pretty late in the afternoon. Not a glowing and romantic sunset—real life here, folks—but still and nice, and the water in the bay is incredibly blue. I sit down in my normal place, a curve of the rock right near where we stuck the ugly little Christmas tree last winter. And Sid sits down on a jutting-out piece of rock that's kind of behind me. And we're talking about some shit or other and laughing and at the same time, I am thinking

Thank you, God, for making this better than the Sisters of Living Hell, when Sid says, "Stop. That's it."

"What?"

"No, shut up, don't move."

I'm sort of turned toward him, so I see him getting out his phone. "What're you doing?"

"I'm taking a picture of you that shows how you really look." He's lifting the camera up and staring at my face.

"Well, now it won't," I say. "And can I just point out that I put up a shitload of great pictures of me looking pretty and you're saying that's not the way I really look."

"Shh. Wait a sec." He's looking back and forth between his camera and me. Intently. That's the word. And then, while I'm waiting a sec, he does that thing where he flops his ponytail behind his shoulder without touching it, and I swear to God I am fucking overcome with lust. I'm talking melting nuclear core. Jesus Christ. Never had that happen before.

Luckily he takes the picture slightly before I become bright red (oh so sexy) and then I can turn around and try to collect myself a tiny bit before he notices. But he doesn't notice; he's chattering away about how boring everyone's pictures are on Instagram, how everyone looks the same. So I am blushing and trying not to, when I hear him say, "You're way prettier when you're talking."

I start laughing (which makes me stop blushing, praise

the lord) and say something like, My orthodontist would be really happy to hear that.

And he says, "No, I mean the way you get animated when you talk. When you take your own pictures, you look posed."

"Of course I'm posed," I say. "That's the point."

"You look better unposed," he says.

I turn around to make a face at him, but inside I'm thinking that it's pretty good, a guy who thinks girls are prettier when they're talking. That's pretty good. And then I see he's looking at me, and I'm looking at him, and I very carefully reach up and pull his ponytail over his shoulder and hold it for a second. His hair is really black and thick. It's beautiful.

I let go.

Silence. Tense, but not Living Hell.

"Will you do that thing?" I ask him. "That thing where you flop it over your shoulder without touching it?"

He looks down at his ponytail and then at me, kind of questioningly. And then he does it.

"Oh," I sigh. "I like that."

Then he leans over and kisses me, and, of course, it's awkward, what else? But nice. Only nice. But that's okay because, really, first kisses between people who like each other—nice is about as good as you're going to get.

Here's the best part, though. While we're kissing—in the

total of six seconds that it lasts—I'm thinking: Oh yeah. Oh yeah. In about four or five months, I'm going to take his hair down. More melting nuclear core. This is going to be good.

"Feel better?" I say.

"Much better," says Frankie, passing the computer back to me.

NOTHING

DATE DUE

**This item is Due on
or before Date shown.**

SEP − − 2017